WEREWOLVES AND WARGAMES

A Spooky Games Club Mystery Book 6

AMY MCNULTY

Crimson Fox
PUBLISHING

"Look, I know how badly you want me to tell you you're out of danger, but face it, my sweet gargoyle—you're in more danger than ever."

Eithne, mostly translucent but every bit the tall, willowy witch I'd known—and clashed with—for far too long, leaned against the spectral form of her companion broomstick, Broomholly, and examined her nails, as if they had any hope of growing or chipping in the realm beyond ours from which I'd summoned her for a chat.

Down the hall, there was a loud shriek of laughter and then a crash, followed by a chittering chirp I knew to be my own companion broomstick, Broomhilde—"Broomie" for short.

"That was me, Your Highness," called Roderick from the other side of the bathroom door. His voice was like that of a very mature ten-year-old's, higher-pitched but full of diction and a stifled sense of excitement threatening to pop out at any moment. "Broomhilde wouldn't stop tickling me!"

That probably meant the crash had been the result of my gargoyle protector turning into his boulder form—a boulder that was getting larger and heavier to carry, I might add, as Roderick himself matured.

Matured.

He was two months old, technically.

Broomie couldn't adjust to the fact that just a few weeks ago, after his confidence had been bolstered because he'd helped me in my second fight against the witch royals who were after my life, he'd started maturing a bit more rapidly. Tickling was the only way she could guarantee to make the little budding stone man laugh these days.

"'Your Highness'?" cooed Eithne, a devious smile curling her thick lips.

"Don't tease me, 'enchantress,'" I muttered, referring to the fancier title for "witch" Eithne had insisted she be known as while she'd been alive— when really, it had just been a fancier way of distinguishing herself from her estranged family. I massaged my temple. "I've been asking him to call me 'Dahlia' or 'Mom.' He used to—well, when he spoke at all. He's taking his role as royal protector very seriously the past few days."

"As he should." Eithne nodded, the words full of conviction in her Irish lilt. "Your mother and I can't help you anymore. Frankly, we should have sought a gargoyle guardian out for you earlier. I suggested we make a golem ourselves. But Cinnamon…" She took off her lilac, pointed, witch's hat, and a lengthy lock of her silver hair fell down over her face.

"Mom wouldn't let you?" I guessed.

Eithne sighed and shook her head. "Always had a soft spot for the things, she did."

"I imagine so. Since my father was one." I tried not to grit my teeth. Things were still tense between Eithne and me—but I'd summoned my mom for advice from that realm beyond the maximum amount of times her soul would allow. Now, if I wanted to speak to either of the two women who'd raised me—in their own ways—I was stuck with my aunt only.

Never mind the fact that I had killed her. She'd wanted me to and hadn't left me much choice.

Water under the bridge now.

"She was too soft on her protector," Eithne said. "Just like you." Broomholly soared around in the light from my rune circle in the den, one of the only spots where the two spirits could appear in this realm—and only then for limited summoning sessions, requiring time between each session before they could make the journey again.

"Roderick is a boy," I said, my back straightening. "I don't want him focused on protecting me—"

"He's a royal protector," Eithne said. Broomholly flew by and knocked into her hat, taking off with it on her bristly head, flying as high as the rune circle would allow.

"I have Lien," I said. My witch cousin—my mom and Eithne's cousin, really—had grown up with the three royal witches after my life. My grandmother, Isadora Poplar, the Queen of Witches, and her two sisters, Sally and Mabel. Mabel was Lien's mom.

"Hmm, yes," said Eithne, crossing her arms. I knew her feelings on the matter, so I finished her sentence for her.

"'She'll help me defeat my grandmother, but when it's down to just me and her, she'll take me out, too.' I know how you feel about her, Eithne. But I don't agree with you. Lien is a good witch."

"There are no good witches." Eithne laughed, and with the cackle that left her spectral throat, the tips of her hands and feet started fading, vanishing back into that place beyond. "Why do you think I called myself an 'enchantress' in my last few decades? Witches have a bad rap."

"My mother was a good witch," I said, even knowing she'd always agreed with the plan for me to be tormented by my aunt and then have me kill her. At least it had been to build up my strength. That was sort of good.

"Aye, and you are, too," Eithne said, a flash of something pained shooting across her eyes. "Just remember—you destroyed Isadora's broomstick.

She may be weakened, but she'll also be more enraged than ever."

"You said her sisters might see this as their chance to inherit the crown," I told her, chewing my lip.

"That I did." With finesse, Eithne grabbed her fading hat from Broomholly as the ghostly broomstick soared by and put it back on her head just as the last parts of her hands disappeared. "But before either can be a queen, they'll have to get rid of Isadora's last remaining direct heir, too."

"Me," I said with a sigh. There really would be no peace until all three witches were stopped.

Eithne shrugged as her shoulders faded. "But you'll get a great big boost of magic if they take out Isadora for you first, and all her power transfers to you. Win-win if you sparked some infighting."

"Lien thinks that maybe they'd rather wait for me to take Isadora out for that reason—pounce the moment I get a boost in power, before I have a chance to get used to it."

"So she recommends you take out Isadora's sisters first," Eithne said.

I clenched my jaw. That was precisely what my cousin wanted me to do. I was being bombarded on all sides with orders to kill witches, and all I wanted was to be left alone.

If not for Cable Woodward being out there, halfway across the world, I'd be perfectly content here in Luna Lane, a small town witch living a small town life. I had no wish to be a queen or princess or anything.

The literal backstabbing involved in witch politics was not at all to my taste.

Of course, now I had no choice but to remain in Luna Lane. In January, I'd learned my lesson the hard way to bide by Lien's orders to remain in the protective bubble she'd cast around the town. No witches could enter the town besides her. That left Isadora and her sisters at a distinct disadvantage.

So long as I didn't mess things up royally and leave the protective barrier again.

"Be careful," said Eithne. Broomholly beside her was only a little bit of wooden shaft. "Trust no one but your royal protector and companion broomstick. And don't rest easy."

"Yeah, I got that," I told her just before she vanished, the rune circle's glow sizzling out. "No resting easy for Dahlia Poplar. Always cursed in one way or another."

I stared down at my left arm, as if expecting to see gray scales there. But those had cleared up months ago, what felt like ages ago. Now I could turn my entire body to gargoyle stone on command.

Well, I was still working on the "on command" part, but it was getting easier each time. I'd so far been able to rely on it twice when fighting Isadora and her sisters.

That was one power my "diluted blood" gave me that those witches didn't have themselves.

Roderick, maintaining his more human-like form for longer and longer these days, trotted down the hallway, heading for the kitchen. Well, he looked more like a moving stone carving of a ten-year-old boy than a human boy, but it was more convincing than the stout, fanged traditional gargoyle form he'd preferred his first month here. His skin was gray, as was his short hair and even the whites of his eyes. He'd fashioned clothing out of his stone self, so those were gray, too—a little suit with tie because he was taking himself very seriously these days.

"Are we out of orange juice?" he asked as he opened the fridge.

The question snapped me out of my thoughts. "Oh, um, maybe?" I only bought it for him, so I hadn't been paying much attention. Actually, I wasn't used to fully stocking my fridge and cupboards. If I didn't feel like cooking, there was always the town's diner, run by my best friend, Faine Vadas, and her husband. Becoming a parent of sorts to my gargoyle was still taking some getting used to.

Of course, the fact that he was talking like a little gentleman just two months after I'd brought him into existence would have conflicted with any parenting advice the other parents in town could offer me.

"We're low on groceries." Roderick sighed and shut the fridge door just as Broomie soared from down the hallway and wrapped her knobby, wooden shaft around Roderick's shoulders, shaking her bristly head in evident excitement. She knew what he was about to say next. "I'll go to Vogel's."

"You have school to worry about," I told him—he'd just enrolled this week. Luna Lane's school was an all-grades-in-one-classroom deal since there were only so many kids in town. That helped, since I'd had no idea where to start him. He was a fast learner, though.

"I'll go, Your Highness," he said, patting Broomie's bristles. She loved a trip to Vogel's, as she was always on the hunt for cornhusks, the only food she ate. "And Broomhilde will come with me. We shall not be long."

"Roderick, I can do it while you're in school. And it's 'Dahlia.'" My face flushed. "Or you called me 'Mom' a few times—"

"You'll forget something." Roderick screwed up his brow and shifted his little business suit to change into a puffy, stone winter jacket. For a moment, a bit of color—navy blue—flashed through the material and his eyes lit up with excitement before the color faded back to gray.

He still had work to do to be able to keep himself consistently at more human colors to be able to blend in better with a crowd. Not that he had to worry about that in Luna Lane.

"Vogel's is right across the street," he said. "It should take me only a short while."

"Okay, if you're sure," I told him. "Put it on my tab. And tell Goldie and Arjun I said 'hi.'"

Roderick turned to me and put one arm across his chest, clacking his stone feet together and bowing. "I will." He paused. "Mother."

My breath caught in my throat, but before I could respond, he was out the door.

I knew he wasn't a little grownup entirely. He still loved playing with the Vadas kids, but it just seemed that the past few weeks… he'd been too eager to demonstrate how mature he was.

He didn't have to be that way.

What was it Faine had told me about raising kids? *"The days are long, but the years are short?"* With Roderick, it was more like the months were seconds and I was about to send the boy off to college before I'd even wrapped my head around the fact that I'd created him.

I had only a moment of silence in the house— and I wasn't sure I liked that, since Broomie had always been my companion before Cable and Lien and Roderick had come into my life—before my normie smartphone rang.

I was getting better about making sure it was always within earshot.

"Coming!" I shouted to it, only realizing a second later that the phone couldn't hear me.

Cable was the only one who called me, other than the devious collection of people called "Spam" everyone had warned me to ignore, and he was requesting a video chat.

I tilted the phone screen just right in the light to get a quick look at my reflection—pale complexion, green eyes, a rather narrow face—and patted down my red, wavy hair. I wasn't wearing my trademark black witch's hat with purple band yet, but I had on my short-sleeved black dress, golden belt around the waist. Yes, it was February, but witches didn't need to worry about feeling too cold or hot when an enchantment was just a few words away.

"Good afternoon!" I said to Cable as I accepted the call.

"Good morning." He smiled back at me, a dimple appearing on his cheek. He was a professor of American literature at a Scottish university and spent a great deal of time indoors, but he had a rather rugged complexion. Dark, short hair that was growing a tad too long, which made more waves appear throughout. Large, brown eyes with long eyelashes I could make out from even behind his glasses. As usual, he had on a tie with a dress shirt that barely contained his monumental biceps. My professor boyfriend had to have a home gym stashed somewhere, but I'd never really seen him obsess over working out.

"Do you have time to chat?" he asked, grabbing a stack of papers on his desk at the university and evening out the pile by tapping them on the hard surface.

"Sure, Roderick went to Vogel's, and then I'm taking him to school. What's up?"

"Nothing." He cleared his throat and narrowed one eye on me. "Just making sure you're safe."

"I'm *fine*," I said. I didn't want him to worry about me. He'd already expressed regret about going back to Scotland after his sabbatical had let him come live with his elderly uncle in Luna Lane last fall. He had commitments to his school—and he'd be free to reexamine those commitments after the semester was over.

We could work with that.

If only my pesky relatives weren't coming to kill me.

"I haven't left town," I said. "I swear. And Lien and Draven are taking turns patrolling the border— there hasn't been a peep of concerning activity." I'd repeated this every day since Cable had found out about my adventure to Creekdale, the neighboring town.

I'd had good reason to go, though. I'd been trying to clear my ex-boyfriend's name.

Speaking of…

"Draven and Lien, huh?" Cable asked.

Draven had never been a fan of Cable. Cable had kept his opinions on the vampire to himself.

"Yeah…" I scratched my temple. "I didn't expect that. Draven is already planning something big for Valentine's Day, judging by his not-so-subtle bragging at Spooky Games Club."

Braggart Draven was annoying, sure, but it was lightyears better than depressed Draven. I was happy my friend was finally moving on. I just hoped it was for the right reason and not because both his vampire sister and I had coupled up with our respective significant others and left him all alone.

But that was his and Lien's business—and finding something besides protecting me to focus on was sure to be good for Lien, too.

Cable sighed, and I did a double-take. Was the thought of Draven moving on a disappointment for him?

"I'm sorry I can't be there for our first Valentine's Day together."

Oh. I hadn't even expected that. It had been so long since I'd done anything romantic for Valentine's Day—and to be fair to Draven, my one and only boyfriend before Cable, if you don't count a childhood crush and first kiss, he'd been pretty good at making it a special day.

"Can't be helped," I said. "Besides—oh, I just found this out yesterday! I haven't told you yet."

"What?" Cable asked, pushing his glasses up.

"Well, the day before Valentine's Day, Faine and I have always had a Galentine. You know, movies, a board game or two, some of her amazing pastries, while Grady stays with the kids."

"Sounds fun." Cable smiled. "I should have known the two of you would play games even before you established Spooky Games Club." He sighed again. "I miss Games Club…"

I didn't want him to dwell on everything he missed about Luna Lane. He couldn't just give up his career after dating me a handful of months.

"Well, this year, she wants to delay it. They're expecting a full house."

Cable cocked his head. "Someone's paying a visit?"

"Half the werewolf village up in Canada is paying them a visit! Well, slight exaggeration. But Faine's parents, Grady's parents and siblings and one's kids, and a host of aunts and uncles and cousins and… I don't even know. To tell the truth, my eyes kind of glazed over by the time she got to the seventh name."

"Huh. Have you met them before?"

"Well, Faine's parents, of course. I grew up around them. And I'm sure a lot of them came to the second wedding celebration Faine and Grady held in Luna Lane." Just so I could attend. Since I hadn't been able to leave Luna Lane, then, either— and I actually couldn't even if I'd *wanted* to then. Eithne's barrier around the town had been about keeping me in, hidden, and it had only been undone by her death. Much stronger stuff than even Lien's work.

"Well, that'll be fun," Cable said.

"I'll say. We could use some fresh faces around here." I winced when I saw Cable's face fall. "I'm really looking forward to it," I added quickly, perhaps with more emphasis than I'd meant to add to my words.

He pursed his lips and stared down at the phone, which he picked up from a stand and started tapping his fingers on. "Isn't the full moon this month on Valentine's Day?"

I nodded. So it was. We were about to have a host of werewolves descend on our town—during the week when they'd all become a bunch of wolves.

"With so many family members, I doubt Faine and Grady will need much help with the kids," I told him. "The pack can keep them in line." It wasn't like any of the kids would go around biting off people's limbs like little Falcon had last fall.

That had been a special circumstance.

Cable nodded, but he did so slowly, as if thinking. "I hope so. But, Dahlia?"

"Yeah?"

"Be careful. Even a seemingly friendly face can bite you when you least expect it."

That was the second time I'd gotten that advice today.

Chapter Two

I wondered if the ground on Valentine's Day was typically coated in snow in Scotland. It sure was in Luna Lane this year—because the day for lovers was a day away and the forecast called for more cold temperatures following this blizzard we were getting this evening.

Faine and Grady's families were supposed to arrive today. Then again, they were from Canada. They were surely used to driving in worse.

I was doing all I could as Luna Lane's de facto witchy plowing service, but my magic extended only as far as Lien's barrier would allow me to travel.

Though, thanks to Lien, the job was getting done in half the time. I'd half-expected her to turn her nose up at the concept of witches riding their broomsticks above Luna Lane's roads and blasting a "TLEM WONS" enchantment along the town's roadways—something I'd done on my own ever since I'd needed to take over for my mom eleven years prior. But Lien, as giddy as a schoolgirl, had agreed, the two of us splitting the town and planning to meet up near Faine's.

Or near Draven's, in Lien's case, I was sure, as Draven was the werewolves' neighbor.

Broomie chirped from below me, her bristles shaking off another light dusting of snow. "Almost finished, girl," I told her, waving my hand and repeating the enchantment again. The road in front of town hall was already cleared, and I was tackling the sidewalk. The snow was almost over—no sense in plowing long before then, unless someone requested my escort service because they had somewhere they needed to be—but the enchantment should stick to keep it all off the rest of the night even if it kept piling on.

Maybe longer. Ever since Eithne's… demise, I'd found my enchantments to have greater reach *and* longer staying power.

Broomie shook her bristles faster than she needed to just to shake off some blowing snow, and I looked down. Mayor Abdel, the mummy, and his great-great-many-times-over granddaughter, Chione, were exiting the town hall after a late night working. Or they'd just waited for the witchy plow service to make its way past so Chione could drive her grandfather home in his polished, red classic Ferrari. They stopped and waved. I waved back. With his mummy bandages covering up every ounce of his flesh exposed beneath his tan business suit, Mayor Abdel was a little hard to spot amidst the blowing snow.

Night was falling and if I didn't finish up soon, I'd have to cast a glow enchantment at the same time or hope the streetlamps were enough to guide me. I only had a couple more blocks downtown to go, and then I could double back and head toward Faine's.

I passed the funeral parlor and was surprised to find Lazarus, the skeletal funeral director, out for a walk. He'd already been out a lot last month, and try as she might, Ginny, our resident ghost, couldn't get him to join us for Spooky Games Club on Saturdays. Ah. There she was now, floating arm in arm with the well-dressed skeleton. He paused, looked up, and tipped his top hat toward us. Ginny beamed and waved, soaring up into the sky to join us.

"How's it going, Dahlia? Broomie?" she asked. Her voice had a hollow echo to it, but it wasn't so frightening with her bubbly tone.

Romance was certainly in the air in Luna Lane.

"We're almost finished with downtown," I told her above the gust of wind and the vibration of my enchantment traveling from my free hand to the road below.

Ginny smoothed out her ghostly, straw-colored hair, clutching a hand to her chest. She wore a tank top with spaghetti straps. "I'd almost forgotten about the snow. Since Lazarus and I aren't affected by it."

Just looking at her made me shiver. I paused in the plowing while I reached the end of the block and did a quick "MRAW" enchantment directed at myself and Broomie once more.

Ginny sighed dreamily and floated beside us as we made a loop and went back again. "Isn't he just so fly?" she asked as we approached the skeleton in cape and top hat, clutching a walking stick, waiting for her return.

Right. She'd been young in the 1990s. I would assume that made some sort of sense to her.

"Enchanting," I told her, pasting on a smile. I still couldn't get the image of his frightening, dark eyes out of my head, even if he couldn't help himself when he'd threatened me.

There weren't many paranormal creatures who frightened me. He was one of them.

"Well, I best be getting back to him," said Ginny, her smile fading as she pouted. "Spindra's shop is around the corner, and we know how *she* is with all the men in town. Faine better watch all her visiting kinsfolk, I say." Ginny tapped a finger to her lips, shifting from worrying about Luna Lane's resident spiderwoman stealing her beau to another topic entirely. "I wonder if any of the visiting were-wolves will be cute."

"Don't let your reaper boyfriend hear you say that," I told her. I shivered as we neared him.

"Oh, he's not the jealous type," Ginny said. "I've got enough of that for the both of us." She giggled and soared back down to the sidewalk. Lazarus nodded at us once more and continued escorting his ghostly sweetheart around the corner.

A few minutes later, I passed the sheriff's office. Closed during the day. Hard to get used to—but Sherriff Roan Birch could only work at night now.

Last month, the fifty-something-year-old normie man I'd thought of as a surrogate father had become a vampire. Qarinah, Draven's adoptive vampire sister, had moved out from the vampire manor and moved in with her new husband.

And vampires had to be in their coffins between sunrise and sunset. It'd taken some getting used to seeing the two coffins laid out in Roan's basement, next to the power tools and the stacks of boxes and the artificial Christmas tree propped up in the corner. At the vampire manor, the basement was virtually empty but for the coffins. It made their sleeping quarters seem more regal somehow.

Then again, Roan and Qarinah's setup seemed cozier. Homier.

It was like Roan hadn't changed. Except I could never see him during the day. I hoped not having any law enforcement half the time never came back to bite us. True, I'd taken a stab at solving more than one crime over the past few months, but I wasn't interested in taking the job myself.

Not too long later, Broomie and I finally made

our sweep to the road leading to Faine's house. At the other end of this very same road, Lien approached on her companion broomstick, Broomhelen. An enchantment shot from Lien's hand, erasing the snow on the road below her as they approached at a steady pace.

I seemed able to go a bit faster. Being the first in line to the witch throne did seem to have a tangible boost to my powers, even if Lien was far more experienced in all manners of witchcraft.

"Phew!" I shouted as I pulled back my hand and met Lien halfway. We were right in front of Draven's and Faine's homes now, Draven's a three-story Gothic Victorian style with turrets, all extra quaint with a blanket of snow. Faine's two-story house was just a bit shorter than Draven's overly large home, but it was cozier, and there were pink and red lights arranged in a heart shape currently blinking from the front window.

"That was a bit of a workout," said Lien as we both approached the ground. There was a broad smile on her face, though. I'd never seen Lien smile so much as she had the past few weeks. She shook out her limbs as she landed at the edge of Draven's driveway, her dress, boots, and witch's hat all in bright orange and making her stand out like a beacon in the snowy surroundings. Her long, black hair was tied to one side in a single ponytail, and snowflakes from the blowing snow landed on her dark eyelashes that framed her almost-black eyes. "You do this every snowstorm?"

"Yeah, the past twenty years. My mom started it, and she had me help out when I was old enough. It's a lot easier when I have someone to help me. I did *ask* you to help me last month…" I frowned as Broomie and Broomhelen shot out from our hands and giddily flew in circles around one another, like two dogs eager to play. Broomhelen always acted more like a dog than a cat, I thought, despite the fact that she housed a cat's soul after its ninth cat life just like every other broomstick. Her cherrywood shaft and furrier-looking bristles made her easier to see in the snow than the paler Broomie.

Lien waved a hand at me. "I was busy. With the barrier." She sighed dreamily as she stared at the vampire manor. "But Draven thinks it's a good idea if I schedule relaxation, you know? Or any other activity to take my mind off of things. And he's right. I feel stronger. And it's not like any witch could get past the barrier without me knowing."

I bit my lip. This was all stuff *I'd* told her last month before she'd started dating our resident single vampire. She'd brushed it off, belittled small town Luna Lane life. Made her excuses that she'd been *too busy* protecting me to help with things like snowplowing.

If this was what love did to a grumpy witch like Lien, all the better.

It'd improved grumpy Draven considerably, too.

Perhaps the two grumpy beings were indeed made for one another.

Eithne was wrong about Lien. I knew that much.

The front door to Faine's house pushed open with a squeak. "Hey, ladies!"

My best friend, all wrapped up in a vintage red, woolen coat, complete with giant, black buttons, headed down the front step of her porch, two steaming mugs in her hands. The blowing snow landed on the red kerchief she'd wrapped around her dark hair, the bold colors of that and her bright-red lipstick popping against her pale-white skin.

"The kids all got hot chocolate, so I thought I'd bring you some," she said.

The two broomsticks stopped flying in circles and shot straight toward the werewolf we met halfway down her drive. She laughed. "I have some cornhusks stashed away for you both from tamale night at the café."

Without hesitating, they zipped in tandem toward her still-open front door, slamming it shut behind them.

"Well… Hello, to you, too, girls." Faine smirked.

"Thank you," said Lien, taking one of the mugs from Faine. She shivered and took a quick sip, the tip of her tawny nose growing red.

"MRAW," I said, waving my hands over the three of us.

"Thanks," said Lien, smiling at me, her eyes

flicking over my shoulder back to the vampire manor. "I forgot to renew that enchantment." She pursed her lips. "I don't remember when I last renewed it. It may have been a while." As she was talking, she grabbed the second mug from Faine's hand and took a sip from it, too, mugs in both hands now. Faine and I exchanged a glance. The one strange behavior solemn Lien ever exhibited was a tendency to drink from other people's drinks when she was nervous. "I've probably been cold for the last twenty—oh! The sun has set." She shoved both mugs at Faine, and the werewolf, clearly amused, accepted them back. "Tell Broomhelen where she can find me. Excuse me."

Before either of us could say anything in response, Lien was down the driveway and moving around to the neighbor's, making her way up to the front door. She pulled a key out from one of the pouches at her belt—never mind that she could have used an enchantment to unlock the door, I think she liked that she had a key—and disappeared inside.

"Come in. Let me get you another mug," Faine said, lifting both mugs in her hands. Some of Lien's lipstick stained both. I hadn't even known Lien *liked* to wear lipstick.

"Oh, it's fine," I said. "NAELC." Picturing the cleaned mugs in my mind, I waved my hands and the stain dissolved. I accepted one mug and took a sip. I didn't know how it worked on germs she might have left behind in the hot chocolate, but we were family. What was a virus or two when we had enchantments—and failing that, Doc Day—to take care of whatever ailed us?

"Roderick did all his homework?" I asked her as we approached the porch.

"He and Flora were finished long before Fauna," she said, referring to her eldest and middle child respectively. "Only hot chocolate motivated that girl to finish reading her picture book."

The house burst into laughter and squeals the moment I stepped inside. Broomie and Broomhelen were flying over the living room, cornhusks dangling from both of their brush heads, while Falcon, Faine and Grady's three-year-old son, and Fauna, their six-year-old daughter, were chasing after them, jumping in the air to try to snatch the bits of dangling fiber out of the broomsticks' mouths.

"Let them eat!" boomed Grady's deep voice. "Your hot chocolate's getting cold."

Grady was standing over the kitchen table, Flora, their newly-turned eight-year-old, sitting beside Roderick, the both of them cradling mugs. Roderick didn't *have to* eat or drink, but he liked to, and he usually opted for sweets. Across from them were two mugs left unattended, a coloring book open between them and crayons spread out across the pages.

After dumping the contents of the mug she was carrying into the sink, Faine put the mug in the dishwasher and picked up a nearby towering block toy comprised of LEGOs stuck together, a sticky substance resembling maple syrup affixed in clumps on one side. "Grady, I asked you to pry this apart."

Grady fluffed a hand in the air. "I'll get to it. Falcon's forgot all about it." Flora and Falcon were currently still running around the house, demonstrating just that.

Faine didn't even look at her oldest daughter as she fluttered around the house, pulling out junk drawers, but she was clearly addressing her. "Flora? Did you take it again?"

Flora stiffened, clutching her mug with both hands.

Grady patted his daughter's shoulder. "I may have left it in the garage."

Faine ignored him. "Flora, I *told* you you're not old enough to play with that unsupervised—"

"A butter knife will pry it apart," Grady said, but he had to speak loudly to be heard as the younger children ran back to the table. The three siblings reunited, I thought to myself not for the first time, how much they looked alike. They all had their father's wide, brown eyes and brown complexion, though theirs was perhaps a shade lighter. Their light-brown hair was thick with curls, which Fauna kept in puffy pigtails on either side of her head. Flora had been getting interested in her mom's vintage style as of late, and she wore a silk, green kerchief like a headband through her dark, voluminous hair. Falcon's curls went wildly left and right whenever he giggled.

"*Anyway*, hi, Dahlia. Thanks for clearing the paths." Grady shuffled into the kitchen, a tall, thin man who at the moment had what looked like snow or baking powder over one clump of his black, close-cropped hair.

"Just in time for your visitors, I hope," I said, sliding my mug onto the breakfast bar counter and taking a seat at one of the stools there. I checked over my shoulder to make sure Roderick didn't need anything, but he and Flora were having some kind of quiet conversation, the werewolf girl nodding as the gargoyle spoke, his back perfectly straight as he sipped his mug like a businessman and his coffee. Both looked like they were playacting being adults, while the little ones were moving their crayons wildly across the pages of the coloring book they shared.

Whatever they found fun, I supposed.

"Oh, they'll come," said Faine, slipping into the kitchen and dropping the LEGO toy back on the counter where she'd found it. "Snow doesn't mean much to werewolves."

"Or Canadians," joked Grady. He was Canadian born and raised, unlike Faine, who'd grown up here in the Midwest. But both her parents had come from the same village Grady had.

Almost as if on cue, the sound of one vehicle after another after another turned our heads, headlights flashing through the front windows and past the blinking pink-and-red heart-shaped lights.

Fauna shrieked. "Grandma and Grandpa!"

"Nana! Papa!" added Falcon.

They both scrambled for the door.

"Hold on!" said Faine, rushing to follow them. "Don't go outside without your coats and don't—"

But the door whapped open, and Grady rushed out of the kitchen to follow them.

Broomie soared by and Broomhelen followed, but not before stopping in front of me and tilting her brush head.

"She's at Draven's." I explained.

Broomhelen nodded, her bristles rustling, and shot out the front door.

Broomie lingered in the doorway, letting all of the cold air in.

I got up, just about to tell her to close the door, when a series of shouts halted my steps.

They weren't the happy squeals of grandkids reunited with grandparents.

These were angry shouts—and more than a few growls.

Two of the cars were still running, both of the driver's-side doors wide open.

And like shadows in the night, flittering back and forth in front of the blaring headlights, two large figures were grappling with one another.

Chapter Three

"Hey! No fighting in my yard!" Faine shouted. Beside her, Grady held back the two of his children who'd darted out, growling in the direction of the grapplers.

A man and a woman, hands locked together, both baring their teeth at one another, turned their heads as one toward the house. The paler woman flushed—I could see as much as my eyes adjusted to the headlights—and the darker-skinned man cleared his throat. They dropped their hands and stepped back.

One of the open car doors was ringing until someone turned the ignition off and dimmed the lights.

"Serafina," said a woman who stepped out of the vehicle. She was tall and willowy, with short, black hair and a pale-brown complexion. Her cheekbones were sharp, her brow prominent.

"What did I say about controlling your temper this visit?"

"Yeah, Mom." A male voice stole my attention. It was familiar, warm. "Way to ruin the trip."

"Echo!" said Faine, her face relaxing. She ran toward the car as a burly man brought a couple of bags out from around the trunk and dropped them to the ground to give her a hug.

The tension seemed to have dissipated as the other car still running shut off its lights and turned off. Grady walked over to the man who'd been grappling with Serafina as another woman came up beside him. Grady spoke to both with arms crossed.

"Papa!" shouted Fauna, giving said man a big hug.

I blinked, taking in the crowd, which was growing larger as more people appeared from within one of the three vehicles—two sedans and a van—and started gathering near the front porch, bags in hand.

"Great-Aunt Serafina and Papa are at it again?"

I whipped around. Flora hovered to one side of me, squeezing past. Even though Flora was plenty tall for her age, at five-nine, I towered over her and she fit perfectly under my extended arm in the doorway.

"I suppose so," I told her.

She shivered and turned around. "I'm going to wait inside. Enjoy a little more peace and quiet before they all come in." Roderick milled about behind us and she directed him back to the table, where they sipped at their hot cocoa.

They had the right idea, but all I had to do was cast another "MRAW" enchantment. Still, I fixed my black shawl over my shoulders and held a hand out for Broomie as I headed down the front steps.

There were a lot of werewolves. There were no inns in town, though Doc Day's boarding house served as the closest equivalent, and I wondered if they were really all planning to cram into the Vadases' home.

"Dahlia! You look… cold." Jonathan Dixon, Faine's father, held his arms out to me as I approached and I gave him a hug. He was bald, round, and on the shorter side, coming up to my chin. His gray handlebar mustache got tangled with Broomie's brush head as he pulled back. "Broomie! Good to see you, too!" he said, laughing as he tugged a bit on their conjoined bristles.

"Be gentle with her," said Frieda, Faine's mom. She helped get the werewolf and broomstick untangled and then offered me and my companion broomstick a hug as well. She was shorter than her husband and her daughter both, pale and hourglass-shaped like her daughter, with short, dark-brown hair in a bob, the color nearly lost amidst all the white now.

She patted her husband as she leaned back. "And you know Dahlia doesn't get cold. Not with her warming enchantment."

"Well, if ever a winter night threatened to break through my enchantment, it's tonight," I added, chuckling.

Despite finally having ventured into other places a couple of months back, I was really awkward at this. I wasn't used to large numbers of people.

"Grandma! Grandpa!" Falcon trotted over, and just as Frieda scooped up her grandson, Fauna plowed into her grandpa and got scooped up by him, too. He chuckled as he groaned and made a big show of how big Fauna had gotten, but there was a slight wince to his features that made me certain the strain wasn't all a joke.

"I apologize for my sister," Frieda said over the top of Falcon's head. "I told her if she couldn't keep things peaceful, she needed to stay home—"

"But then where would all the fun in that be? Everyone knows a family reunion always needs a little drama." Echo, the cousin Faine had hugged so enthusiastically, sauntered over to our little group and sniffed, a wide smile on his face as he put down the bag he was carrying and extended open arms. "Dahlia? Looking witchy."

"I'll take that as a compliment," I said, accepting him back. I studied him as we let go. "Looking… wolfy."

"Thanks." He ran a hand through his shaggy, brown hair. He was more muscled than I remembered, amply filling out his white Nordic sweater that washed out his lighter complexion.

Echo was four or five years older than Faine and me, and she'd always looked up to him as an older brother. He'd visited a number of times when we'd been growing up, usually without his parents, who'd been going through a rough divorce, I remembered. His dad had even moved to Europe, last I knew, and his mom had gotten remarried. It'd been a few years back, and Faine had told me all about it when she'd returned from the werewolf village up north.

"I hear our little witch is taken again, Echo," said Frieda as she set Falcon down.

I cocked my head at her as Echo grinned, leaning forward and whispering behind a hand. "Aunt Frieda keeps trying to set me up with any woman who crosses my path. Good thing you have your vampire. Hey, bud." He leaned down to ruffle Falcon's hair before the little kid ran back to his parents.

Broomie nudged me with her bristle head.

It'd taken me too long to figure out what they'd meant—Echo thought I was still dating Draven.

"Actually, Draven and I—"

"My gal, Broomhilde G. Broomstick!" Echo said, offering a high five to my companion.

She leaned forward, tapping her head to his open palm.

I laughed. "What's the 'G' supposed to stand for?"

"'Greatness,'" Echo answered without flinching. "Or maybe 'Goober.'" He ruffled her bristles and let out a mock-scream when she shook rapidly, running away as she shot out from my hand and chased after him.

Mid-thirties and still that teasing older teen brother at heart, I see.

Faine was speaking to her aunt now—Serafina. I'd only seen her a few times, despite spending weeks at a time with her son as a kid. That meant the woman who'd admonished her was Cinder, her wife, at least a decade her junior. I didn't think I'd ever met her before. Neither Serafina nor Cinder had made it to Faine and Grady's second wedding in Luna Lane.

"Dahlia, you remember my mom and pop?" Grady's voice drew my attention as Frieda and Johnathan allowed Fauna to lead them inside the house, balancing their bags. "Kodiak and Wisteria Vadas."

Kodiak dropped his chin to his chest and offered a brief nod. He was tall and bald, a patchy gray-and-black beard neatly trimmed drawing the eye to his prominent jaw. "Good evening," he mumbled.

Wisteria slapped a hand across his chest. She was also tall, her close-cropped white hair popping out against her dark complexion. There was a scar down one cheek and over a brow, but it made her even more beautiful somehow. "Please excuse him. He's doing his best to mind his manners. Nice to see you again, Dahlia." She extended her hand and I took it, meeting her gaze. One wide, brown eye, and one fogged over, like with a cataract.

"Oh, it's—it's nice to see you, too," I finished awkwardly. I really wanted to ask what that tussle had been all about. I'd met them at the second wedding and during one or two visits since.

Grady picked up Falcon and looked over his shoulder. There was a group of people by the van's open hatch whom I hadn't even taken note of yet. "We're heading inside!" he shouted.

He started in after his in-laws, and Faine took note and motioned for Serafina and Cinder to follow her as well. I was about to go after them when Broomie zoomed overhead, and I reached out to grab her.

"No fair!" shouted Echo. He skidded past in the snow in the yard, shaking out his head like a wild dog. "I'm 'it.'"

Wisteria's lips went into a thin line as a growl rumbled in Kodiak's chest. "Aren't you a little *old* for tag, Echo?"

Echo stood and straightened his sweater. "Some of us like to stay young at heart, Mrs. Vadas."

Before she could reply, someone approached from behind the back of the van, his eyes narrowed on Echo.

He didn't growl. He didn't say a word. He just stared at him.

Echo coughed and straightened up, heading inside with quick strides without a word.

Wisteria smoothed down her jacket, which may have gotten bunched up on the long car ride. "Dahlia Poplar, witch of Luna Lane, this is King. King Bane."

If that wasn't a name that seemed to suit the man, I didn't know what did.

He was older—maybe in his sixties—but he towered over everyone around him. Nearly as broad as he was tall, he looked positively *jammed* into his puffy, black winter coat. His complexion was only a shade or two lighter than his dark coat, and though he was bald and bearded like Kodiak, his white beard was longer than Grady's father's, giving him a sort of grumpy, super-in-shape Santa Claus look.

I definitely would have remembered him if I'd met him before.

"A witch, huh?" King said, giving me a quick onceover. His voice rumbled with an almost-musical note. "Bet with a witch in this town, they don't have trouble with trespassers like we do back in the village."

"Trespassers?" I echoed. I didn't want to explain we sort of *did* have a problem with trespassers— murderous witch ones out to get my life. Faine had assured me she'd warned everyone, though.

"Enough of that," said Wisteria. "Petra! Inigo! What's taking so long? Let's get inside."

A couple of teenagers approached, but I knew they were not Grady's siblings, whom she'd just called out for. One was a boy of about seventeen years of age—pale brown and a dead ringer for Falcon grown older, I'd wager, down to the curly, brown hair. He was practically swallowed up by his puffy, blue coat. The other was due to be about fourteen, if I remembered right. A short and skinny olive-skinned girl, her dark hair in braids with a single golden chunk woven into the braid that now clicked across her face.

"Nyko and Milah, do you remember Miss Dahlia?" Wisteria asked.

It wasn't lost on me that King took Kodiak aside as she made the introductions, keeping a hand on his shoulder and whispering to him.

"No," said Nyko. He was staring at a smartphone and hadn't even looked up to check if he remembered me.

Milah smiled awkwardly but said nothing.

"Nyko, *put* that thing away—" Wisteria started.

"Mom, I got it." A woman I recognized to be Petra, Grady's sister, approached with a couple of bags dangling off each arm. She was tall, like the rest of the family, almost enough to be a model, but she kind of disappeared into the fluffy, tan coat she was wearing. She looked a lot like her daughter, down to the hairstyle, though her braids were pulled back into a bun that rose up above her head. "Nyko, I asked you to help your uncle with the bags."

"I said I *would*. I'm texting Julie. You know—the *girlfriend* you *forced* me away from during our first Valentine's Day."

Dumping the bags at his feet, Petra reached across her son and snatched the phone away. "And I *told* you enough was enough. You texted her the whole trip!"

Nyko's nostrils flared as he stared at the phone in his mom's hand. "I didn't even want to *be here.* You could *at least* let me talk to my girlfriend."

Petra snatched the phone out of his reach, as with her high-heeled boots, she towered over even her son. "If your father were here, you wouldn't *dare* speak to me like that."

"Yeah, well, he *isn't,* is he? He's always traveling for work. Whatever." Nyko grumbled and picked up one of the bags in front of him, groaning as if it weighed one thousand pounds. "Why doesn't *she* have to help?" He glared at his sister, who stood there silently—staring at Broomie in my hand, I realized.

"Why don't I lend a hand?" I offered. "I could use an enchantment to make the bags levitate—"

Petra shot me a look that could kill and I bit my lip.

"Nyko, if you want to stand out here in the cold and sass me some more, I suggest you dig out your rabbit-fur hat because you and I, we are going to be out here *a while* until you do as I've asked you. And you're not going to get to answer any of your texts the whole while." The phone she was clutching buzzed, as if on cue.

"*Okay,*" Nyko grumbled, suddenly finding the

strength to snatch the rest of the bags and sliding them over his arms. He shuffled inside the house. When Milah found me looking at her, catching her still staring at Broomie, she jumped and scrambled after her brother without another word.

Petra sighed and slipped her son's phone into a pocket in her oversized coat. "I am sorry, Dahlia, but—"

"No, I'm sorry. I was just trying to be helpful. I should have realized more was going on." At the rate Roderick was growing, did I have this kind of attitude to look forward to in a month or two?

I wondered how his little budding crush on Flora might work if he outgrew her in the blink of an eye.

Or maybe I was assigning something more to two kindred spirits finding they enjoyed each other's company.

"Deep breathing, sis. Deep breathing." The van beeped as one last visitor strolled up behind Petra.

Inigo Vadas. Grady's fraternal twin brother who wasn't identical but still looked alike in virtually every way—though Grady now had some scars on his arm I hadn't been able to heal when I'd reattached it after a bit of a werewolf... incident.

Petra rounded on him. She had an inch even on her brothers, but maybe that was just the heels. "*Deep breathing?* Inigo, when you have a teenager of your own, you can dole out advice, but until then—"

She cut herself short as her mom nudged her with her elbow.

Inigo's face fell as he shifted one of the two bags he held in his hand over his shoulder.

"I'm sorry," whispered Petra. "I didn't mean—"

Inigo swallowed and brushed past her, nodding at me. "Dahlia. Long time."

"Y-Yeah," I said, not expecting to be addressed in the middle of whatever heavy conversation was going on there. "Hope you've been well."

He grunted and shrugged.

Wisteria's grin reached her eyes as she nudged her son this time. "Why don't you tell her the news?"

"What news?" I asked, when not a single member of the Vadas family was forthcoming.

Inigo mumbled something and headed inside. Petra swallowed and walked quickly after him as Wisteria called her husband and their friend back over. "Let's get inside!" she shouted. She looked at the house, already bubbling over with sound and activity. "If there's any room…"

The last of us headed toward the front porch, but Wisteria was right. There was quite a backup in the entryway. Bags piled high across a haphazard pile of wet, sopping boots, and Grady's arms were already stuffed with winter coats. Children screeched as Fauna and Falcon were running in circles around Milah, who just watched them running around her, her braids whapping across her face with each turn.

Kodiak stomped some snow off of his boots on an already-sopping rug. "Son, I'm not sure if there's really going to be enough space for everyone."

"Good evening!" bellowed a deep voice from behind him, one with the slightest hint of a Transyl-vanian accent. "Welcome to Luna Lane. If I may, as the neighbor of werewolves for nigh on fifty decades, I would like to extend an invitation."

Everyone still hovering by the door shuffled aside, and I turned around to find Draven, Lien wrapping her arm around him as vampire and witch hovered before the threshold of the open doorway.

Chapter Four

"*D*raven?" I said aloud. The sun had set a short while ago, and I'd assumed he and Lien were off to do a patrol of the barrier together—if they came out of the vampire manor at all.

Draven smiled broadly, revealing his sharp incisors before running a hand through his wavy, shoulder-length blond hair. The leather of his black jacket rustled as he moved.

He looked like a rocker from several decades back—all black leather, partially exposed chest—except that his skin was deathly pale, his eyes a shining red.

He gestured to the threshold of the open door.

"Oh!" said Faine, no doubt remembering a vampire needed to be invited into a home not his own each time he entered. "Please, come in, Draven."

Everyone shuffled back into the cramped space even more, and I brushed up against a werewolf somewhere behind me as I stepped back.

After Lien, Broomhelen soared in and shut the door behind them, using her brush head to grab the handle.

Draven clapped his hands together and looked down at his new witch girlfriend.

I wondered if witches were a type with him.

Then I chastised myself for even thinking that.

They were good with each other. Two grumpy souls made far less grumpy when combined. I just hoped it lasted.

"Lien heard about the visitors coming today and thought your house might be a bit..." He looked around at the crowd packed together in the living room, dining room, and kitchen. "Cramped."

King let out a guttural sound somewhat like a growl, but Kodiak elbowed him and shook his head.

"There are all sorts of paranormals in Luna Lane. That's one of the reasons why my son wanted to move here. One of the reasons." He nodded at Faine.

Faine shuffled forward and gestured to the latest two to enter her home. "Everyone, this is Draven, our neighbor. And this is Lien Poplar, Dahlia's cousin."

Echo did a double-take, looking at Lien and me. We didn't look anything alike, unless you counted our similar taste in attire. That was because royal witches apparently "tried out" different fathers for each of their children.

And eliminated the fathers of the previous children before they found a new one.

I tried to keep myself from gagging at the thought of Eithne's stitched-together resurrected father I'd met on the train.

But familial resemblance wasn't what was actually on Echo's mind, apparently.

"You dumped Dahlia for her cousin?" he remarked.

Faine's jaw dropped.

Lien blinked rapidly as Broomhelen draped around her shoulders. Draven thrust his chest out and wrapped his arm around Lien.

"I did not 'dump,' as you say, anyone. Dahlia and I have been just friends for many years." His eyes met mine. It was true enough, though it wasn't so long ago that he'd been moping about me dumping him many years before. And getting more upset once I'd started dating Cable. "Lien is now my paramour."

Lien's eyes widened as her body froze. Then her cheeks darkened and her shoulders slumped. She seemed surprised and embarrassed—but happy.

"What's a paramour?" Flora asked from the dining room table.

Grady shushed her, though Johnathan chuckled under his breath. Frieda elbowed him.

"In any case," said Draven, "my paramour"—

oh, this was going to become a whole thing now with him, wasn't it?—"suggested that, as my home is emptier now than it's ever been, I offer rooms within it for any of your friends and relatives who care to join me." His red eyes flashed over King, who clenched his fist at his side while staring down the vampire, and even Draven flinched a bit, swallowing. "It's a bit dark in the house, but Lien cleaned it with her magic."

No one spoke for a moment.

"Well," said Faine, "that's mighty generous of you, Draven! I didn't even think to ask—"

Because the vampire never would have offered such a thing before.

"Vampires aren't allowed to feed on anyone without their consent in Luna Lane," I blurted out, drawing the eyes of everyone in the room. I shirked back. "If... you were worried about that."

"I thought I heard about a vampire who did just that," said Inigo. He crossed his arms over his chest and jutted his chin toward Draven.

Draven offered a pinched smile. "My sire. She's been punished appropriately."

"I heard that, too." Inigo nodded. He glanced around the room. "Very well. I'll take you up on your offer. I figure it's about time I get used to working with vampires anyway."

"Inigo," said Wisteria softly as he bent down to grab his bag.

He squeezed her arm. "I'm just putting some stuff over there. I'll be back for dinner."

"Wonderful!" said Draven, though he didn't offer any explanation about Inigo's desire to work with vampires, either. Perhaps he was equally confused. "Any other takers?"

King darted a glance toward me and I jumped. Only I realized with a start that he was looking *past* me. I turned around to find Serafina and Cinder.

"They're staying, I'll go," he said, despite his clear misgivings about Draven just moments before.

"I reckon we should too," said Kodiak, looking at his wife.

"*Dad*," said Grady.

"We'll just be next door. Right?" Kodiak asked Draven.

Lien whispered something to Draven and Draven nodded. "I won't be able to feed any of you, unless you stop by my sister's and my pub, First Taste, next door to Hungry Like a Pup. But there's plenty of room for your luggage, and I have nothing but guest rooms, considering I don't use any of the beds."

I'd never actually spent much time on the second floor and above of his manor, not since Draven and I had dated all those years ago. I'd never really understood why Ravana had furnished any of the other rooms, considering they'd all slept in coffins in the basement. But if I remembered right, the place was only about half-filled with furniture on the upper levels.

Kodiak and King shuffled back toward the door, putting on their boots and avoiding the wet spots on the ground.

"YRD," I said, waving a hand at the puddles on the floor.

The wet spots evaporated.

King and Kodiak stared at me, and King *tsked*, shaking his head.

"All right, all right," said Wisteria. "You boys can take my things over there, but I am *not* leaving this house yet." She shuffled past Grady to get to Flora at the dining room table, bending down to kiss the top of her head.

Roderick stiffened at the action, and Broomie seemed to notice—she flew out of my hand and landed around his shoulders, as if offering him a hug no grandparent ever would.

"Well, thank you, Draven." Faine clutched her hands together and cleared her throat, exchanging a wide-eyed look with Grady, who just shrugged. "I hope you'll join us for the special Spooky Games Club event."

"What's that?" I asked. Such a thing was news to me.

"We just decided we'd ask your club," said Grady as Inigo, King, and Kodiak stepped outside. Grady wasn't in our club, though he and the kids joined for some games of their own on occasion. "To join us at our Valentine's Day wargame."

Some poet somewhere would revel in the oxymoronic taint of that phrase—making some point about love and romance being akin to the battlefield, no doubt.

I was just confused.

Draven chortled, an echoing laugh, and Lien joined in. She was new to the Games Club the past few weeks, never having cared for such frivolities before.

"What's a wargame?" Lien asked.

The room took that as their cue to resume their conversations, Grady's family picking up bags and pointing to one another and putting on formerly wet boots. Nyko was summoned from his spot sitting on the staircase to help with the bags again, I noticed—with a great big sigh that carried over the noise of the room.

Echo nudged me from behind. "You're not with the vampire?"

"Yeah, I tried to tell you earlier. My boyfriend is a normie."

"Where's he?"

"Scotland."

Echo raised an eyebrow. I was trying to pay attention to Grady's explanation, but Echo seemed more interested in my love life, apparently. "Online dating?" he ventured. "Faine said you only recently got a phone."

"That was *because* of the boyfriend. No, he's Milton Woodward's nephew. And he visited for a few months last year."

"Ah. I see. When you can't go to the world, let the world come to you."

I nudged him back, smiling despite the somber fact he was relaying there. "I lucked out, I guess."

"You know, I'm glad you and the vampire split. I always thought he was too emo for you."

"'Emo'?" I asked.

Draven and Lien were listening to Grady with rapt attention. He did sort of look like a goth guy with his girlfriend dressed like a witch for a Halloween party.

Draven nodded at something, ran his hand through his hair, and then shook his head once, as if he'd just washed it.

"Well… He is a bit dramatic," I admitted.

"And you seem to have a good head on your shoulders." Echo crossed his arms and studied the room. His mom and step-mom had stepped away, talking with Frieda and Jonathan closer to the dining room. Falcon and Fauna approached them, leaving Milah alone in the kitchen. Flora got up to talk to her, her back to me, as she tried to get Milah's attention.

The teenager was staring over Flora's head at Draven, though, her mouth open in just a little "o."

Draven *was* the sort of bad boy a young teenage girl often dreamed about. I was so glad I'd never really interacted with him much before I'd turned twenty-one. Who knew how desperate I might have been to date him before I'd gotten that good head on my shoulders.

Flora finally managed to get Milah's attention, though, and the older girl looked down at something Flora was showing her, but I got distracted when Echo elbowed me again.

"What's with the stone kid?" Echo asked.

"The 'stone kid,' as you say, is Roderick. My gargoyle protector." I cleared my throat. "I've only had him with me a few months, but he's like a son to me."

Echo leaned back and gave me a long onceover. "Look at you. Dahlia's all grown up. Dating foreign men—"

"He's American, just abroad."

"Raising a kid—"

"Well, I mean, he grows super-fast, so sort of."

"Having a target on your back?"

Echo's gentle ribbing had gone cold.

"Yeah," I said softly.

"Faine told me. She might have mentioned your new gargoyle, too, but it slipped my mind. Or I guess I didn't expect to find a little gentleman version like that." He chewed his lip.

"I feel bad about having you all come when I've got some witches after me," I said. "But Lien's barrier should keep them all out."

"Oh, I'm not worried about that. With all of us here, I'd like to see anyone even *try* to hurt you."

A wistful smile crossed my face. It did feel a bit safer having a sort of big-brother type like Echo here for at least the next week.

My smile vanished and my voice lowered. "What was with your mom and Kodiak?"

"Oh, that's nothing." Echo fluffed a hand in the air. "They've been fighting over their territory for ages—they have neighboring plots back home. Werewolves don't get surveyors out to demark land or anything. It's more instinctual than that. And Kodiak, he's never seen eye to eye with my mom about it. Been a problem since I was a teen."

I cocked my head. "*Because* of you?"

"Well, maybe." He chuckled. "Mom's on my side, though, says the lands I've hunted on have been my dad's for ages. He up and abandoned the place, so it's Mom's and Cinder's and mine now."

I didn't question that he was still living at home with his moms in his thirties. I knew werewolves were more open about that than many normies in these parts. Packs were packs.

"But why fight the moment they pulled into the driveway?" I asked.

"I didn't hunt on disputed lands before we hit the road or anything, if that's what you think. I'm not *that* foolish." He winked. "Frankly, I've let the whole area be for years now. Tired of all the grumbling. But the Vadases, on the whole—they still don't like me."

"Why?"

He shrugged. "I've been asking myself that for decades. Not even sharing any of my hunting bounty satisfied them. They were angry I'd stepped even a *toe* onto 'their' lands." He rolled his eyes. "No, the thing just now—back in Creekdale, we made a pit stop. I know we were close then, but Milah had to go." He nodded at the youngest visiting werewolf, who seemed to be in a grim conversation with Flora. Or maybe she was just trying to pay attention as the younger girl rambled.

"I was taking a nap in the car while at the gas station," he continued. "I woke up to Mom shouting, and Kodiak shouting back at her. Cinder and Wisteria got them back in their cars, but Mom wouldn't talk about it. She just seethed the rest of the way." He shook his head. "Then as soon as we parked, the two of them were going at it like no time had passed at all." He sighed. "It's a good thing your ex invited some of them to stay at his place, I say."

"Can't you all talk it out?" I asked. "You're all here to visit *family*—"

"We're all here for the wargame," he said succinctly. He rounded on me, his brows drawn together. "And if you're scared of getting hurt, you'll stay out of it—whatever Faine and Grady say. Were-wolves don't *play*."

Chapter Five

With Roderick at school, Lien's protective barrier up and keeping any new witches from entering the town, and Cable far away, I was left with little to do. Add Ginny being so caught up in her new romance and Faine being busy hosting family to the mix—and even Sheriff Roan becoming a nighttime-only citizen of the town—and you might even say I was bored.

I fell back on old habits and asked people around town if I could lend a hand, doing my "good deed" for the day since I didn't have a job. Mom and Eithne's fortune left behind in another dimensional space, which Cable had helped me turn into American currency in a bank in Creekdale, took care of the need for that, but there were only so many odd jobs one witch could do in a town of three hundred. It'd been a problem when my life had more or less depended on accomplishing a daily do-gooder task.

After I'd enchanted away the snow on all the crosswalks and driveways still unshoveled around town this morning, Mayor Abdel had sent me on my way.

"Warm yourself up with a hot coffee," he'd said, clearly forgetting I had enchantments that could do the trick faster and more efficiently. "And rest up for the Games Club special meeting tonight. I wish Chione and I could make it, but I don't think me traipsing around in the dark in the woods is a good idea. Not at my age."

Several thousand years old, I was pretty sure.

He'd been right, though. Hungry Like a Pup's hot coffee was warming me up better than a warming enchantment could do.

Broomie let out a little bristly sigh that was hard to mistake as she chewed absentmindedly on a cornhusk. Broomie never ate cornhusks with anything but gusto.

But I knew the feeling. Despite the bustle in Luna Lane's sole restaurant—well, outside of the food they furnished for the pub next door—we felt kind of set apart here in the corner booth. It was Valentine's Day, and everyone else had somewhere to be, something to do. I was itching for a task to take my mind off my Valentine being halfway across the pond.

"Should I call him again?" I wondered aloud. Broomie listlessly turned her brush head toward me. I checked the time on my smartphone, which I'd remembered to bring with me when I'd gone into town. No, Scotland was six hours ahead of us. He'd be getting ready for bed by now. He'd read me poetry this morning during our Valentine's Day Facetime date. His deep voice had given a rhythm to the lyrical sentences that had made me feel as if he were truly speaking to me, even through Maya Angelou's words and not his own. I'd never pictured myself as a fan of poetry until this morning.

I blushed at the memory and took one last long gulp of my coffee to cover it. Though no one other than Broomie was even looking my way.

Behind the counter, Frieda was helping Jeremiah, the farmer who lived outside of Luna Lane and provided most of the fresh crops when he had any to the eatery and to Vogel's store. The farmer laughed, his wide, dark eyes lighting up as he scratched his hat and jostled his mostly gray hair. It'd been a while since Frieda had paid a visit in person, and Jeremiah was about the same age as her and her husband.

Back in the kitchen, Jonathan was humming and cooking up an array of to-go orders on top of everything ordered by the few other groups in the dining establishment. Some of the more reclusive citizens came out for special occasions, the ones who didn't seem to get caught up in any of the trouble that happened around Luna Lane. Normies, anyway. Most of the paranormals were pretty actively in my social circle.

Erik, who worked with Mayor Abdel at town hall, was having a Valentine's Day lunch with his wife. She was much taller and paler than he was, but there was something to the matching colors they wore, the similar amount of gray in their dark hair, that made it seem like their long marriage had made them grow more and more together.

I wondered if, one day, Cable and I would look like that to someone nosily people-watching like I was.

Or if his career—and my secret—would keep us apart.

I still hadn't told Cable about me being a witch royal. It hadn't seemed important when I'd explained Isadora's desire to end me having to do with my "tainted" blood in her family.

I hardly understood the importance of a Witch Queen, anyway. Eithne and Lien had said there wasn't a witch castle anywhere or anything, and it wasn't like Isadora ruled by levying taxes and proclaiming laws, so what was the point?

Other than the transfer of power to the direct royal line, I supposed.

Still, the longer I went without talking to Cable about it, the more it felt like I was *hiding* something from him, when I just didn't want to give him more reason to worry.

Draven and Lien knew. A lot of people in town knew.

But he wasn't in town anymore. Not lately. So why add to his stress?

The front door jingled as Jeremiah shouted, "Take care!" and left with his order in a paper bag in hand. Lost in my own thoughts, I hadn't even noticed him walk away, or Frieda currently headed to my table.

"Phew," she said, sitting down in the booth across from me after one more quick look around the restaurant. Everyone seemed caught up in their meals and conversations. "I miss it, but I don't miss it, you know?"

She scratched the side of her head real fast, and I could almost picture a dog doing the same with her hindleg. You got used to little bits of doggy behavior slipping in around werewolves, especially as the full moon approached.

"I'm sure Faine and Grady appreciate you giving them the day off," I said. Broomie nodded and floated on over closer to Frieda. The werewolf couple were headed over to Creekdale for a quick movie matinee before the kids got out of school.

"Those kids deserve it. They work too hard." The older werewolf laughed and pet my broomstick's shaft. Floating, Broomie arched her shaft like a cat's back into the pets. "I just forgot—Valentine's Day is one of the busiest of the year. Not sure if Jonathan's and my old bones can handle it."

"You look great," I said. "Need a refresher?" I waved my hand around in the air.

She chuckled. "Please."

"LAEH," I said, waving my hand in her direction. For a second, I'd been tempted to take away her sensation of pain, but I'd learned my lesson the hard way that that just caused more problems. "YGRENE."

"Ah." Frieda visibly relaxed as my enchantments did their work to soothe sore bones and muscles, at least temporarily. "Thank you."

"You sure you don't need my help?" I asked, not for the first time.

She fluffed a hand in my direction. "You were shoveling all morning. Take a minute to relax."

I'd been here half an hour already, cradling my cup. "I used enchantments—"

"Which are just as draining in their own way. Don't belittle your own accomplishments, Dahlia. Embrace this advice from your Auntie Frieda." She leaned over the table to look into my empty mug. "Do you need a refill?"

I shook my head.

The front door opened with a jingle and we both turned, Frieda about ready to get up, but as soon as she saw her sister, she sat back down, hollering toward her fellow werewolf. "Jonathan's in back. Help yourself."

Serafina nodded, a scowl making the movement seem terse and ungrateful, and walked past the counter and through the doors leading into the kitchen.

Frieda winced. "Actually, maybe I *should* charge her since this is Faine and Grady's place now, not mine. Force of habit. But she's been in such a terrible mood lately. I'll add cash to the till myself."

Broomie curled up in Frieda's lap, twisting herself in a circular shape. I opened my mouth to tell her that Frieda had to work, but the werewolf lifted a finger to her lips as she pet the broomstick, her long nails getting caught in the bristles a bit. "I'm on break," she said. "I'll check in with the other tables in a minute."

I stared back into the kitchen. Johnathan had been scraping something off the grill and he turned to face Serafina, who crossed her arms and spoke softly.

"I don't remember your sister visiting much when I was growing up," I said. There was still something to Echo's warning that worried me, even if Faine had invited the rest of the Spooky Games Club to participate in tonight's wargame and didn't seem the least bit concerned.

"No, she didn't. She had a rough time after her ex left."

"That's why you watched Echo for weeks at a time," I said.

"Gave her time to find herself. Find a way to support her boy as a single mom." Frieda shrugged. "I don't know. She didn't really seem to finally get her act together until she met Cinder, and poor Echo was already grown by then."

"Cinder got Serafina to calm down pretty quick last night."

"She's a good influence on her. The yin to her yang." She nodded softly. "She joined our pack a few years back. She's from a pack farther out in Nova Scotia, originally. Said she was looking for something new. Probably hadn't meant to stay, but she and Serafina fell in love, and that was that."

I swallowed. Somehow, the thought of romance upending someone's plans for themselves made me queasy. I just knew I'd feel guilty if Cable ever gave up being a professor for me—but I didn't want to leave Luna Lane, either. Not in the long term.

For now, though, I didn't have a whole lot of choice in the matter regardless.

"Echo said his mom and Kodiak used to fight over property lines."

"Oh, Kodiak is such a stickler for those. He's the only werewolf—well, other than King—who cares about such things. We're supposed to be a community." Frieda scrunched her nose.

"But why were they fighting last night? It wasn't like he caught her or Echo trespassing right before they left and held it all in until they got there, right? Echo mentioned a break you all took in Creekdale."

"I couldn't tell you." Frieda *tsked*. "I didn't notice anything out of the ordinary until Serafina leaped out and charged at Kodiak. I mean, Inigo *did* say something to Echo at the gas station, but…" She drifted off.

"What?" I asked. Echo hadn't mentioned that. My amateur sleuth instincts—or my boredom—were driving me to get to the bottom of this.

Call me nosy. I'd admit to it.

"Well, about five or six years back…" Frieda looked over her shoulder and then leaned over the table, her petting of Broomie, asleep on her lap, forgotten. Her voice softened into a hush. "Echo and Inigo, they fought over the same woman."

That wasn't where I'd expected this dispute over trespassing and property lines to go. "Five years ago?" I prodded. I hadn't heard about either having a girlfriend or getting married, so I assumed it would have been old news by now. Not enough to start their parents at each other's throats last night, certainly.

Frieda bit her lip. "Lexa Bane. King's one and only daughter—only family since his wife passed."

"Oh." I could feel my pulse pounding at the gossip. "Faine never mentioned that."

"Yes, well, I never liked the woman, to tell you the truth. It's shameful of me to say about a member of the pack, but there it is. She was nothing like her mother. Good woman, Jasmine Bane. Sorely missed in the community."

Pushing aside my mug, I leaned on the table to get closer to her.

"Lexa dated both Echo and Inigo," Frieda whispered. "And tried to keep it a secret from the other. Told them both she was trying to keep her love life a secret from her overprotective dad, but really, she was just leading the boys around by their noses." Her lip curled. "Even Serafina didn't know about it until the big incident."

"Incident?" My voice was a harsh whisper.

"Lexa got pregnant." Frieda paused, allowing the news, which had shot my eyebrows up to my hairline, to sink in. "Told Echo it was Inigo's. Told Inigo it was Echo's. And then told both boys to take a hike, and she left the village."

My jaw dropped. "She… *left*?"

"King knows where she is, but only King. He's mum about his grandchild, at least to us. Maybe he tells the Vadases everything, I don't know. He's practically an older brother to Kodiak. I'm sure he'd rather Inigo be his grandchild's father. But still, Inigo hasn't gone anywhere. Hasn't seen this kid that I know of. Maybe he believed her when she said it was Echo's. Maybe she had a *third* man she was messing around with on the side." Broomie stretched out the tip of her shaft like a leg or a tail. "Still, King loves his girl so much—I have no idea why he didn't move wherever she went. To be with her and the baby. Well, *kid* now."

The door to the kitchen swung open with a *bang* and Serafina stormed out, no to-go bag in her hands. She marched past the counter and headed out the front door, not even acknowledging her sister as she passed.

"Is she all right?" I asked.

Frieda rolled her eyes and started sliding down the booth. "Serafina's gotta be Serafina about everything," she said. Broomie got the hint and moved off her lap, scooching around and settling against my thigh.

As Frieda stood, I grabbed her wrist before she could leave. "You said Inigo said something to Echo? At the gas station?" I realized it was a bit weird of me to grab her like that and dropped her arm.

She didn't seem to mind, though. "I don't know what. I just noticed the raised voices. Those two have been so cold to one another since the whole situation. We'd hoped they could work out their enmity with the wargame."

"Yeah, about that. Echo hinted it could get dangerous."

Frieda laughed. "Werewolves talk tough. But ever since we added paintball to the ritual—not an easy task when in wolf form, I might add, but you'll see that tonight if you're coming—there haven't been any significant injuries. Just a little bruising here and there.”

I arched a brow. Well, I supposed even normie paintball games, from what I’d heard about them, could result in similar injuries.

“I should definitely come, then,” I said, though I’d always planned on it. “I imagine it’s too late in the day for Doc Day, and my enchantments can heal any bruises from overzealous incidents pretty easily.”

“That they can,” Frieda said, rolling her shoulder. “I might even stand a chance of helping my team win tonight with you on hand.”

The front door opened and in stepped Inigo, and I did a double-take. First recognizing who he was—he did so look like Grady, I mistook him for a second—and then realizing what he was wearing.

“Already his first day?” Frieda said. “You would have thought he’d take a day or two to get adjusted. And wait until *after* the game.” She spoke louder. “I’ll be right with you, dear.”

Inigo nodded and headed up to the front counter, looking up at the menu hanging above the open window overlooking the kitchen.

“First… day?” I asked.

Inigo Vadas was wearing the outfit I’d only ever seen on one Luna Lane resident before. A tan-colored uniform, complete with utility belt and weapon, and a matching tan ten-gallon hat.

The overhead light gleamed off his shiny, gold sheriff's badge, too.

"Didn't your sheriff or Faine tell you? I heard he turned vampire—so he reached out to the werewolf village and hired Inigo for Luna Lane's daytime shift. It was Grady's idea."

No, they hadn't told me. No one—not my surrogate father, not my best friend—had told me anything of the sort at all.

Chapter Six

"MRAW," I said before pulling my hands back and pointing the enchantment at myself, even though I wasn't due for a renewal of the warmth enchantment.

"Force of habit?" Sheriff Roan Birch chuckled as he affixed his paintball vest. The Vadases' van had been carrying all the equipment necessary for the game.

"Yeah," I admitted. Broomie was over by the Mahajans, whom I'd just warmed with the same enchantment. Goldie was wrapped up in a puffy, purple coat that popped amidst the snow-covered field, her black-and-silver hair pulled back into a bun under her knit cap. Her husband, Arjun, had a matching blue knit cap over his balding head and was decked out in a dark woolen coat that practically reached his ankles. I wasn't sure it was suited for the wet snow, but he probably had never pictured he'd be out playing in the snow at his age. Not without his grandkids visiting.

As Broomie floated overhead, Roderick was in his stubby gargoyle form on the ground beside the Mahajans, passing out vests and goggles to his team with a grim look on his face, like he was about to head off into real war.

A vest appeared in front of me and I grabbed it. Roan had been handing it out for our team—we'd drawn lots and my little gargoyle guardian was on Team Red, while I was Team Blue—and he passed one to his wife, Qarinah, who had just finished adjusting goggles across her face.

Both were vampires, though in Roan's case, that was a recent development. Pale complexions, dark hair—more full for his part than it had been lately in Roan's normie life—and red, glowing eyes, just like Draven. Cold didn't bother the undead, but they'd both still made an effort of sorts, wearing matching green tracksuits. Qarinah's did little to hide her hourglass figure, but she still looked sporty with the vest and goggles on, her long hair pulled back in a ponytail that swished back and forth every time she moved her head.

"Mayor Abdel and Chione were going to come, but then he thought he might have too much trouble seeing in the dark. They're waiting with Lazarus back at Faine's house to see if we want to play any other games afterward. Well, without the werewolves." I slipped my vest on, affixing the Velcro in place on either side of my torso. "Milton wanted to come," I told them. He, like the mayor and his granddaughter, was a member of our Spooky Games Club, though he suffered from dementia and was rather advanced in age. "But Ingrid told him it'd be too cold. She convinced him to stay home and watch romance movies instead."

Roan chuckled. "I bet she teased you plenty about your first Valentine's Day with her son." Ingrid, the constant traveler, had initially planned to stop by for a month or so to see her brother and son, but perhaps seeing her brother's condition first-hand had finally convinced her to stick around. Milton enjoyed the company.

"Well…" I blushed. "But it's not *really* our first Valentine's Day together. He's not here."

"Next year," said Roan, and he gazed at Qari-nah, who winked at him. "You two kids will have next year."

Well, since I was thirty-one, I was hardly a "kid," but to Roan, perhaps I'd always be. Even if he now looked my age or younger.

"Meet you at the starting line," Qarinah said, a hint of her Middle Eastern accent punctuating her words. She was all-business as she picked up a paint-ball rifle. It resembled a real rifle, which I wasn't too crazy about using around kids, but it had a bunch of orange plastic fixtures all across the length of it to designate its non-lethality. She slung the strap over her back and headed over to where Ginny hovered, wearing a vest and goggles of her own—not for her protection, but for targets the opposing team could more easily hope to splatter. If she focused hard enough, her body could become corporeal in parts, which was how she held her own paintball rifle.

As the vampire approached, Ginny waved her over to where the blue paintball ammunition was stockpiled, beside a makeshift little hut some of the werewolves had built earlier today from sandbags, old tires, and planks of wood. A single wolf patrolled back and forth, though the game hadn't begun, protecting our stronghold with the yellow flag the opposing team would be aiming to capture. In the distance, you could see Jeremiah's house at the edge of his farming fields, a cozy fire lighting up the place and sending smoke out of the chimney.

Team Red's stronghold was deeper in the woods off to the west of ours, at a similar little hut. We'd all been given a tour of the sites by Grady in his large, gray wolf form, trotting proudly back and forth, so we'd get a better idea of how to plan our wargame strategy.

The werewolves were all wolves right now, the full moon shining overhead, making the snow below sparkle.

Falcon and Fauna were the youngest wolves, their wild temperament still sometimes a problem I helped out with each month, but they had been improving.

And now, their brown-furred Dixon grandparents in front of them, they were actually falling in line like wild wolves in a pack. The wolf I was pretty sure was Jonathan strolled back and forth in front of three wolf cubs I recognized for sure to be Faine and Grady's kids, and the kids stood straight, only Falcon's tapping back leg any deviation from the rigid posture.

Draven and Lien were on Team Red along with them—Faine and Grady, too. The wolves had all managed to slide into protective vests fitted for dogs and Lien was affixing dog-sized goggles to their faces, Draven hovering behind her and making her laugh with what I assumed to be one of his cheesy jokes.

Roan slid two rifle straps over his arms and picked up a box of similar small-sized goggles. He tilted his head toward the Team Blue fort. "Shall we? We're supposed to outfit our wolf team members, I presume. I wonder how they manage it back in their wolf village."

"I think they have some normie caretakers. There're a lot more kids in the village than here, and they need someone to keep an eye out for anyone who escapes out to the normie communities, even if they're fairly remote."

I whistled for Broomie as we walked and she turned abruptly, rubbing the top of Roderick's head real quick as if mussing with his hair, only he had none in his more traditional gargoyle form. His stone nose wrinkled as she flew off across the snowy field and landed in my hand.

More wolves were gathered around our paint-ball stockpile now, and Qarinah and Ginny both were taking turns loading up the small, orange-colored miniature paintball cannons the wolves would each carry.

On the backs of their vests was a place to affix the loaded paintball weapons, and I imagined they had some kind of way to set them off. The strange weapons had no typical trigger or place to light a fuse or anything.

Before we got close enough to be overheard—werewolves retained their memories as wolves, after all—I put a hand to Roan's shoulder. It was cold.

"Why didn't you tell me about Inigo Vadas?"

Roan shifted the contents of the nearby box and handed me a pair of the larger goggles. "I assume you mean Luna Lane's new daytime deputy sheriff?"

"Yes," I said, taking the goggles stiffly. Broomie peered at them as if sniffing them as I let her go and strapped the pair over my head. "I didn't think we needed another sheriff."

Roan sighed and put the box down on the ground. "I'm old, Dahlia," he said, though he looked to be in his prime. Albeit his very pale prime. "And now I can't do anything when the sun is up—

which will be more and more of a problem as spring and summer get here."

"You're not even retirement age," I pointed out. He was in his mid-fifties.

"And I'm not retiring." He handed me one of the paintball guns strapped over his shoulder. "But with how things have been here lately, I knew we needed someone active during the day. We're not such a quiet town anymore."

As if on cue, one of the werewolves leaped on top of Team Blue's makeshift headquarters and howled at the moon.

"Yes, but…" I bit my lip and held tightly to the strap over my shoulder.

Roan leaned closer. "Inigo was a member of the werewolf village's police force—small, but larger than ours, to be sure. He came highly recommended after Grady let him know I was looking for someone." He let out a deep breath, though I didn't think vampires even needed to breathe. "I didn't ask you because, despite the fact that you have the skills, you don't have the training."

"I didn't want to be—" I started.

He held his hand up. "I know. But I don't want you to think I didn't think of you."

That… helped soothe the sting, actually. A bit.

"I just hope you two get along," Roan said. "Give him a chance. That's all I ask." He chuckled. "Well, I *really* hope Luna Lane no longer needs your mystery-solving assistance, but just in case… I let him know how helpful you've been on our cases as of late."

I cleared my throat, feeling my face flush, as Broomie dived into the box of goggles, coming out with several pairs caught amidst her bristles.

"I don't even know him," I said. "I'm sure we'll get along if he's anything like Grady. It was just… a surprise, that's all."

"Well, he wasn't sure until the last minute," Roan added, plucking one of the goggles off of Broomie's bristles and holding it out for the wolf who approached. Roan spoke softer. "I asked Grady and Faine to keep it quiet until he made his final decision."

"I bet Mayor Abdel knew," I pointed out. "And your wife. That means half the town knew—but not me." Slight exaggeration.

"Of course, Abdel needed to approve the budget for the new deputy sheriff. And I wasn't going to hide my plans from Qarinah." Roan smacked his lips together, his sharp incisors gleaming in the moonlight. "I didn't think you'd take it so personally —hey, Inigo." Roan slipped the goggles on the gray wolf who'd sat down beside him.

I grimaced as the wolf narrowed his eyes on me. I hadn't recognized him. And he'd probably heard me.

And he currently had a paintball cannon strapped to his back.

Roan finished affixing the goggles over his eyes and grabbed another pair off Broomie. Broomie, clearly happy to be helpful, dived back into the box to get more out before soaring back beside Roan as they approached the remaining wolves.

Inigo didn't stir, still staring me down, upright and rigid.

I wondered how Roan could even tell that wolf was his daytime sheriff replacement.

I looked back out over our team. They were all gray-furred—varying sizes, but I couldn't tell one from the next. Other than that one howling at the moon. He was the largest, so I suspected he was King.

I counted the wolves wearing Team Blue vests. If I had to guess, we had Inigo, King, Kodiak, Wisteria, Nyko, and Milah on our team—Milah was probably the smallest gray wolf, though she was larger than Flora. As well as Roan, Qarinah, Ginny, and me. Well, and Broomie, though she was more my assistant.

On the other team, I definitely recognized the mixture of brown and gray wolves that were Faine, Grady, Flora, Fauna, and Falcon—and there was Jonathan and Frieda, too. Petra must have been the svelte, gray wolf I didn't recognize next to Falcon, and then they had Lien with Broomhelen, Draven, Goldie, Arjun, and Roderick, too. Three more players than our team, but they had the youngest players, too, and I didn't expect them to be great assets.

But where were Serafina and Cinder?

I looked around. And Echo.

Almost as if reading my mind, three more wolves trotted up to the field from the direction of town, Inigo's growling alerting me to their presence at first.

Two brown wolves—one large, one medium-sized—and a limber, white wolf whose fur practically blended in with the snow.

All three headed in our direction, and Inigo stood on all fours, pointing his nose stiffly as the large, brown wolf I was sure I remembered resembled Echo approached.

"He's Team Blue, right?" I asked Inigo, even though he couldn't respond. "We're all on the same side here."

Inigo's lips curled back, revealing monstrously sharp canine teeth.

Echo trotted past him, his nose in the air, not even bothering to acknowledge him, though he rubbed up against my side.

"Hey, Echo," I said.

He didn't seem affronted, so I assumed I had to be right.

His moms went over to the pile of equipment, and Qarinah, Roan, Ginny, and even Broomie helped them into their vests, goggles, and paintball cannons.

Echo sat down beside me, his tail wagging.

Inigo let out one more grumble and walked away, his padded feet quiet on the snow.

"Don't you need to get ready?" I asked. "Why were you all late?"

Echo cocked his head at me, letting out a little whine, and I laughed.

"I suppose you can't write your replies out in the snow." I swung my paintball rifle off my shoulder. "Let's get 'em, partner!"

Echo nodded his wolf head and sprinted toward the makeshift team headquarters, the last to get equipped for our werewolf wargame.

I lined up beside Ginny as Broomie flew back to me and wrapped herself around my shoulders. Across the field, just at the edge of the woods, the other team was lining up as well.

"Isn't this exciting?" asked Ginny. "I wish Lazzy were more open to fun."

"I can't picture him playing anything other than board games. Card games, maybe."

"He'd be great at this! He doesn't get cold, either, and the paint would splatter nicely over his dark jacket and white bones."

I chuckled. "I thought you said he'd be great at this? The best players don't *get* splattered."

"You know what I mean." Ginny lowered her paintball rifle and the rest of our team lined up. She frowned. "What's with the latecomers?" she asked me, rather quietly for her, I'd have to say.

"Our gray wolf teammates didn't seem too happy with them."

"Yeah, I'm surprised they're on the same team, actually," I told her. "Frieda basically told me the wargame might help them vent their frustrations with one another. Hard to do when you're on the same team."

"Luck of the draw, I guess," said Ginny. We'd both been present when Faine had drawn names back at her house, shortly before the sun had set and all the werewolves had shifted.

But it *did* seem weird. Both of the Dixons and the local Luna Lane werewolves on one side of things. The rest of the Vadases on our team. Well, Petra was on the other team.

That was one anomaly, at least.

And Lien coupled with Draven, Roan with Qarinah, Goldie with Arjun…

Basically everyone who had a spouse or partner in the game had been paired up with them.

But I supposed there had to be a fifty-fifty chance of that anyway. Right? I wished Cable were here to ask. He was a professor of the humanities, but he was pretty good at math, too. I was sure the odds got lower the more you weighed how frequently the couple-pairing had come up.

The largest wolf on the other side—Jonathan, I was pretty sure—howled at the moon from the middle of the line.

I stared down Team Blue's line. I was on one

end of it with Ginny, one of the gray wolves settling on Ginny's other side. In the middle, we had the wolf I assumed was King, and he let out an answering wolf call.

Then silence hung heavily in the air.

And Team Red broke off, running like a coordinated team into the woods.

Chapter Seven

The wolf I suspected to be King howled, and the other gray wolves on Team Blue broke into a triangle formation with King at the head of the line, leaving the brown wolves and white wolf and the rest of us non-werewolves still in a line.

"What's the plan here?" Ginny asked, cocking her head.

Roan let out a roar, and Qarinah followed, both heading toward the treeline after the coordinated formation of gray wolves, their paintball rifles at the ready.

"I guess… go for the trees?" I said. It *was* the obvious plan. I just felt odd to be on a team with a clear, agreed-upon plan that we knew nothing about.

At first I thought Serafina, Echo, and Cinder had been left out of the plan because of the tension between the two families. But Echo leaped up a stack of tires and sat up straight on his hind legs, while Cinder leaped up the sandbags and landed on the roof. Serafina slipped inside the makeshift hut, peeking out one of the open gaps in the planks of wood acting like windows.

"I guess they're on defense," I pointed out to Ginny.

Ginny nodded, chewing her lip. In the moonlight bouncing off the snow, her ghostly-white body seemed to sparkle. "I guess I'll hang back with them."

I would have guessed Ginny would have been more gung-ho about the warfare part of this. But the necklace she wore, once a red-jeweled brooch, a gift from my mother, shone then in the moonlight and reminded me that Ginny had once been so driven to get revenge, she'd nearly lost herself.

Maybe all the shouting and screaming and anger was a little too close to home.

Then again, I thought most of the bad blood was between members of Team Blue. It wasn't like anyone on Team Blue attacking Team Red or vice versa would be filled with any kind of vendetta.

Broomie let out a little chirp as she took to the air and I slung my paintball rifle into a better firing position, adjusting my goggles one last time.

Broomie hovered over my shoulder. We'd discussed it beforehand—aside from the broomsticks, no flying. The vampires weren't to turn into bats to avoid paintball targets, either.

Broomie's presence made me feel a bit less silly running across the snowy field all by myself, wolf pawprints of all sizes in the snow before me.

When I hit the treeline, I found all was quiet. Eerily quiet. Ahead, some of the brush looked disturbed and there were pawprints leading through the snow. I found one set of pawprints I'd managed to follow from Team Blue's side into the woods, so I homed in on that path and went ahead.

A small crack of a branch drew my attention and I spun around, my paintball rifle at the ready.

It was a gray wolf wearing a Team Blue vest.

It wasn't the smallest wolf, but it wasn't one of the larger ones, either.

Whoever it was, they scratched at their chin with their back leg, then sulked flat against the snow, laying their chin down between their front legs, completely unbothered by the fact that I'd trained my paintball rifle on them.

Clearly bored, despite the fact that they'd run into this woods in formation.

"Nyko?" I guessed.

The werewolf rotated one ear toward me, his eyes barely shifting in my direction. His face didn't pick up off the snowy ground, but he seemed to nod even so.

I chuckled to myself. Even as a werewolf, the teenager was determined not to participate.

I'd let him have his secrets. Maybe he'd been posted to this area and his family assumed he was on the lookout for any Team Red members passing by.

Broomie grew almost comically straight and I righted my rifle in the direction she pointed with her brush head. There was soft footfalls coming some distance away and I dived for cover, Broomie sliding under a bush beside me.

Goldie stepped out quietly into the clearing, pointing her rifle down at Nyko.

Nyko shrugged his foreleg shoulders.

"Um, little Team Blue wolf?" she asked.

Nyko's tail whapped, and he made no effort to move.

"Um, sorry about this?" Goldie said. Wincing, she took a step back and shot in his direction, closing her eyes.

The splatter hit Nyko's cannon and vest, leaving a red splotch mark.

Nyko let out a little whine, then what could only be categorized as a *sigh*, as he trotted back toward the treeline and the open field. Still not bothered much at all, if I had to guess. Probably eager to have been taken out of the game as soon as possible.

"Sorry!" Goldie shouted after him, wincing.

I bit my lip. This was a wargame. It wasn't *too* much different than beating her in a board game or a card game, was it?

"I'm sorry, too!" I shouted, popping up and letting my paintball ammunition rip toward her vest.

Goldie screamed and a splatter of blue paint appeared on her abdomen.

"Are you all right?" I whispered.

Broomie laughed, her bristles grinding up against one another, and darted out to rub her brush head against Goldie's face.

Goldie put a hand to her chest and breathed hard, but she seemed to be gathering her breath. "Oh my goodness. You two. That was quite a trap. Sacrificing a wolf? I wondered how I'd gotten so lucky."

It was more of a spur-of-the-moment thing than a trap, but yeah, it had worked out that way. Thanks to Nyko's lack of enthusiasm.

"All right, all right, girl, I'll head out to the clearing." Goldie patted Broomie's head and then Broomie stilled, floating back over to me.

A howl erupted into the night some feet away, followed by a loud *thump* that could only be a cannon going off.

"Good luck!" Goldie shouted after my retreating form. "But watch out for Arjun. He's taking this quite seriously."

I bolted forward through the trees, holding myself back from using any enchantments to clear the way, a twig getting caught on my skirt more than once, and as the second such thin stick scraped across my exposed leg, I realized I really *did* need to start expanding my wardrobe beyond this black dress with an added shawl in the winter, especially if there were situations where I wasn't going to be using any enchantments.

There was a whimper up ahead and a quieter shot than last time. One of the rifles.

"Sorry, little wolf!" Arjun hush-whispered as he fired again. The smallest wolf on Team Blue—Milah—let out a whimper as she bolted my way. She didn't stop to fire back, running willy-nilly with her ears flat against her head.

Arjun let out another shot and Milah only *just* dodged it.

Broomie shook her bristles and nudged at my rifle. I stopped running, taking aim above the wolf sprinting in my direction. Arjun was so focused on her that his eyes only darted up at the last second—too late.

I let out my blue paintball ammunition and hit him square in the vest.

Milah whimpered and kept running, hiding behind me.

"Oh! Oh! You got me!" Arjun dropped his paintball rifle and let out a fake-sounding death cry, collapsing to his knees and reaching for the sky.

Broomie shot up and toward him.

"You got me, Broomie. Dahlia." His voice was harsh as he clutched his chest over the paintball splatter. "Tell Goldie… Tell the boys… Ugh." He fell face-forward.

Broomie shook wildly over our fallen friend, then draped herself over him and kept sobbing.

"It's all right, Broomie—he's just pretending," I reassured her as I made my way over.

She shot up and instantly stopped her cries. Then she bristle-chuckled. Arjun got up and chuckled with her.

She'd been in on the joke, too.

A whimper caught my attention and I turned around to find Milah padding over.

"Sorry I chased you, little wolf," Arjun said. "I got one wolf already and I felt emboldened."

"You got one of my teammates?" I asked.

"A big, gray one. Not the biggest one, though."

Milah hit the ground three times with her front paw, her head lowered.

"Inigo?" I ventured, wondering if the three paw taps meant three syllables. There was Kodiak, too.

But Milah nodded, her ears drooping. I wondered if she'd teamed up with him and had been counting on him to protect her. Perhaps he had.

"He put up a good fight," Arjun said. "I only just missed his cannonball." He shuddered as he got to his knees and, slinging my rifle over my shoulder, I helped him to his feet.

"I got Goldie, sorry," I said. I wasn't very good at these wargames, was I? I just felt *bad* every time.

Arjun let out a deep breath. "I should have stuck

with her. We could have held each other's hands on this cold, snowy floor."

"She's waiting in the field," I said, nodding over my shoulder.

He clasped my hand and gave it a shake. "Good luck out there. I don't know what all those wolves on my team are up to, but I know they're taking things very seriously. Draven is *out* for blood and so is your cousin. You got the lightweights on the team." He winked. "Don't lower your guard yet."

He pushed forward through the brush, leaving me with Milah. I pulled my paintball rifle back into my hands. "Want to stick with us?" I asked her.

She nodded, whimpering.

I nodded back.

Broomie took to the air and straightened again, pointing the way.

I didn't hear anything at first this time—these paintball soldiers were much more skilled than any I'd encountered so far.

Broomie grew very quiet and lowered to the ground, ducking behind a tree trunk. I followed after her, Milah trotting softly on my heels.

I peeked around the tree trunk. There was movement up ahead, something low to the ground I assumed had to be a wolf.

But there was the *thud* of a paintball hitting something from a higher trajectory, too. Rifles.

Only Draven, Lien, and Roderick were left on Team Red using paintball rifles. Roderick had been in his gargoyle form last I'd known, though he wasn't supposed to fly, so I figured his paintball ammunition would come from a lower level.

Of course, this could be my teammates—Roan and Qarinah—in battle against Team Red wolves, too.

And then, in the darkness, there was the shiny glint of red eyes.

"Vampire," I whispered.

Milah whined, and before I could stop her, burst around the tree trunk and whapped the cannon on her back with her tail.

I'd wondered how they'd set the things off.

A blue paintball cannonball went flying through the air with a loud *crack* and something whimpered up ahead.

Another paintball cannon exploded and shot our way. I only just ducked back behind the tree trunk in time.

Broomie shook wildly and Milah groaned, her ears flat against her head as she turned to run. Then, when something clinked out of her vest and onto the hard ground, she came back and bent to pick something up with her mouth before she scattered off in the opposite direction.

"Milah!" I whispered, but she ignored me, rounding a bend and vanishing farther into the woods.

Someone let out a deep battle-cry and ran

toward me. I whapped my rifle out to meet theirs as the combatant came around the corner.

Draven.

We locked eyes.

He hesitated.

Then I shot first—and he shot a second later.

Only just as my paintball hit the target of his vest, Broomie let out a riotous rustling of her bristles and dived between us, catching the red paintball splatter across her bristles and shaft.

"Broomie!" I shouted.

She collapsed to the ground as if exposed to para-paranormal, completely inert.

I dropped my rifle and skidded across rough terrain to catch her, just barely keeping my balance. She hung stiffly in my arms for a moment, and panic rose inside me at the thought that maybe some para-paranormal was nearby to take her para-normal ability to move away. But then she swung more dramatically in my arms, her brush head dangling back. A bit of extra bristles pushed forward like a lolling tongue.

She was play-acting.

Draven put his rifle strap over his arm and *tsked*. "I do not know if it was fair for Broomie to take the shot for you."

Broomie's bristle-tongue sputtered at him.

"Fine, fine." Draven held his hands up in surrender. "You win, Broomhilde."

Broomie let out another little death throe cry and lolled her brush head more.

"Or you lose," Draven added.

"All right, all right." I pet Broomie's head. "Thank you, girl. I won't forget your sacrifice. Now go with Draven to the clearing."

"Yes, I will escort you," he said. Suddenly briefly all better, Broomie jumped up into his arms and he stumbled to catch her. She hung limply across his abdomen, her head lolling down still. "Hey, I am shot, too," he pointed out. She just lolled her head again. "Okay, okay," he said. He winked at me, one red eye going dark. "I would not leave your weapon discarded so long, Dahlia. Not on the battlefield."

Almost as if to make his warning ring true, the most frightening howl I'd ever heard whipped all of our heads in the direction behind Draven. Even Broomie perked up in Draven's arms at that.

Snarling, a giant wolf appeared, his tail whapping his cannon.

I shrieked—then saw the Team Blue vest on the wolf. Based on the size, it was King. "Wait, I got him! And I'm on your side!" I shouted.

But the cannon went off.

I winced and protected my eyes with my forearm out of instinct, despite the goggles.

Then I realized I didn't feel any paint hit me—and there was a rustle up above me in the canopy of trees.

With a grunt, something hard and heavy

dropped to the ground beside me, like someone had thrown a rock.

I opened my eyes to find Roderick in gargoyle form pointing his rifle in the wolf's direction. No flying, maybe, but he could have climbed that tree at any time. Maybe he'd even had his rifle trained on me. Blue paint splattered the tree trunk, and I realized Roderick had been King's target all along.

King bolted out of the way just in time to avoid the shot, then whapped his cannon with his tail again.

The weapon produced a hollow *click*, but no paintball cannonball exited. He was out of ammo.

He growled, his eyes trained not on Roderick— but on me.

Oh, right. I was still in this. I scrambled to pick up my paintball rifle as King bolted in the direction of the field—and our little headquarters fort, where he could pick up more ammo—following the path Milah had broken in the foliage during her own retreat.

Roderick trained his paintball rifle on the mighty werewolf's retreating flank.

But at the last second, he spun it around and fired it at me instead.

I'd only just grabbed my rifle. I hadn't pointed it at him. I'd been too distracted.

And I felt this *force* against my chest like someone had lightly smacked it. Red paint dripped down the front of my dark vest.

Roderick smiled a wide, toothy grin at me.

He was having fun, at least. That much, I could see.

"You got me," I whispered harshly.

Broomie chuckled a bit in Draven's arms.

Roderick just nodded and retreated deeper into the woods, in the direction opposite of King. He wasn't foolish enough to chase after the big werewolf before he regrouped.

Draven grinned, his incisors lowering. "To the field, Dahlia. With Broomhilde and me."

"All right, all right." I got to my feet and slung the rifle strap over my shoulder. I wondered how many people were left on each team and if anyone had even gotten close to capturing the flags. Team Red would have to travel quite a bit a ways around to approach our headquarters from behind. They couldn't do it from the wide, open field. They'd be too obvious, and Serafina, Echo, and Cinder would see them coming.

We walked side by side through the broken foliage, trampled now by two werewolves. Broomie still hung limply in Draven's arms and I was pleased to see he didn't object to carrying her.

"Is Lien still in the game?" I asked, no longer trying to keep quiet. Hopefully, the paintball soldiers would realize we weren't in the game anymore, based on the way we didn't make any attempt to keep our footfalls quiet.

"Last I knew," Draven said. "She's helping to

guard the flag." He let out a dreamy sigh. "She's so good at *protecting*."

I wondered if he meant because she had charged herself with protecting me.

I cleared my throat. "She's… good for you. You're good for her. I'm happy for you two, Draven."

He looked down at me and smiled. His glowing, red eyes made him especially easy to see. "Thank you, Dahlia. I should have been happier for you, too. I *am* happy for you. I just hope you and your professor can find a way to be side by side someday. Like Lien and me."

I blushed. "What happened to your big Valentine's Day plans?" I teased him. "Surely, you didn't mean a special meeting of the Spooky Games Club."

"Oh, the night is young." Draven winked. "I doubt this game will take up the rest of it. Afterward, I plan to take her—" He froze.

"What?" I started to shift my rifle off my shoulder, only to remember I was out of the game.

Broomie stiffened and shot up, no longer playing the dying comrade in Draven's arms.

"I smell blood," said Draven softly.

Someone was hurt? Actually hurt?

"Where?" I tossed the rifle to the ground, eager to use my enchantments.

Draven and Broomie side by side led the way.

Just ahead along the path were two figures. Low

to the ground. A deep growl, a throaty, echoing grumble vibrated into my bones.

A large, gray wolf paced around in a circle, a crumpled-up form on the snow. Red paint had splattered across the fur of a brown wolf—a brown wolf who wasn't wearing a vest or cannon, just the goggles.

Draven hissed. "That's not paint."

What I had mistaken for red paint trickled into the snow around the body of a werewolf.

Chapter Eight

"LAEH!" I shouted, skidding to my knees across the snowy, muddy ground. "Get this off him!" I added.

Draven turned into a bat with a *poof* and then flew toward my side in an instant, reappearing in his human form with another *poof* and then gently removing the goggles from the fallen wolf's head.

The giant, gray wolf I presumed to be King paced back and forth, his tail whacking Draven and me as he neared us.

"LAEH!" I shouted again, shaking my hands over the fur matted with the dark stain. Nothing seemed to be happening.

I could hear Broomie's bristles shaking from above with a soft, almost-cooing sound.

"Dahlia." A cold hand gently landed on my shoulder. "They're gone." Draven reached over to the wolf's eyes and shut them. Just the tip of the creature's tongue lolled out of its mouth.

I touched the wolf's flank. The soft fur. There was no rise and fall of the abdomen. I pulled my hand back and it was stained red.

It wasn't paint.

The large, gray wolf stepped back, jumped up on a nearby rock, and howled toward the sky. The sound was sad, like a lullaby heard only through a faded memory.

It took only a moment for there to be an answering cry. Then another off in another direction.

Broomie nestled around my shoulders, rubbing my cheek with her rough bristles as I stared at the body in front of me and held out my bloodied hand.

I barely registered the constant motion in the brush on nearly every side of us as wolf after wolf, both gray and brown, gathered amidst the dense foliage.

There was a human gasp as Goldie and Arjun appeared together, clutching on to one another, a small, gray wolf by Goldie's side splattered in red paint.

The white wolf darted straight to my side and sniffed the blood on my hands, letting out a whine. She nudged at the fallen wolf below.

Growling drew my attention as a large, brown wolf confronted the big, gray one, only the brown wolf's teeth bared as their lips pulled back.

My eyes darted around wildly, taking note of the glowing, dark and yellow eyes belonging to the canines all around me. I needed to know which wolf this was. Where was Faine? Where were the children?

My heart thumped so hard, I clutched at my vest, spreading blood amidst the brighter red paint there.

A brown wolf appeared beside me, nudging their way in between Cinder and me—and I realized with a start I knew it to be Faine. I saw her as a wolf every month. I knew her.

She sniffed at me, rubbing her head against my shoulder, jostling Broomie, still around my shoulders like a scarf, and shifting her goggles a little bit. I ripped them off for her. She whined and put a paw on the fallen wolf's flank. She nudged them again and again.

Then she threw her head back and screamed— as much as a wolf could scream. It sounded like a scream.

With another growl, a sleek, gray wolf jumped between the brown one threatening the largest gray one and barked at the brown one.

The foliage shifted again and out stepped Roan and Qarinah, followed by Lien.

Qarinah dropped her rifle to the ground, slowly removing her goggles as Lien dashed over to my side.

"Did you try—" she started.

"It won't work." My voice cracked. "The heal enchantment didn't work."

Draven stood and embraced Lien, the woods growing suddenly quiet.

"Everyone, listen up!" Roan handed his paintball rifle off to his wife and removed his goggles as he stepped nearer. There was a red splatter of paint across his vest. "This is now a crime scene, so I'll need everyone to calm down and give us space." He nodded to the gray wolf who'd stepped between the growling one and the one I suspected to be King. "Inigo?"

I stared at the wolf Roan had insisted was Inigo, trying to commit his shape to memory, too. There was nothing in particular to distinguish him from Grady or even Wisteria or Petra, as they were all about the same size. I supposed there was the narrow squint of his eyes—or maybe that was something that wolf only trained on me.

I let go of my vest to stare at my hand. I knew I looked guilty, but Draven, Broomie, and the wolf I assumed to be King could attest I hadn't done this. When Draven, Broomie, and I had approached, only King had...

I jumped to my feet, trying to make sense of everything around me. If Cinder and Faine were here grieving, and then that big, brown wolf who'd threatened King...

A little whine caught my attention. There were

the kids. My heart sunk with relief, though I knew the fallen wolf was too large to be any of them. Grady and two other brown wolves tried to block the children's view of the body on the ground, directing them back, though Flora in particular was keen to see, ducking around and under wolf legs and giving Grady quite a task of trying to block her until he barked—once, harsh, flat. Flora's ears went back and she joined her siblings in the retreat.

If those two brown wolves were Faine's parents, I guessed, and Cinder was here, then…

Cinder rubbed her nuzzle against the brown wolf who'd been growling as another gray wolf trotted up to two smaller gray wolves and barked at each. The smallest gray wolf hung her head and they both fell in line, the three trotting after the others who'd left for the clearing. I was starting to get a sense that that was Petra with Nyko and Milah. Those two gray wolves over by King had to be Kodiak and Wisteria.

Goldie and Arjun nodded glumly at me as they turned to head for the clearing, too.

Only Ginny and Roderick hadn't shown up, as far as I could tell. I did a mental count of the wolves. They were all accounted for. I just wasn't sure if the wolf on the ground was Serafina or Echo.

I pet Faine, who was whimpering, as another brown wolf trotted out from the retreating line of wolves and nudged at Cinder and the other brown. The brown ignored the newcomer entirely and sniffed at the fallen wolf, then threw their head back and howled, my heart breaking at the sound.

A rustle of leaves to my left caught my attention as Roderick burst through, dropping his gun, tossing off his small vest and goggles and transforming into his gray humanoid form, complete with stone winter coat, pants, and combat boots as he appeared at my side. His eyes widened at the sight of my bloodied hand, which I kept clutched out in the air, as if preserving evidence.

"You're hurt!" He didn't sound like the calm and collected little grown-up child he'd tried to be as of late.

"What? Uh, no. NAELC." I gestured at the dirtied hand with the other, and the blood and paint mixed together faded away from my skin and vest. "I'm fine, Roderick."

Roan was directing the remaining gray wolves in the direction of the clearing and Inigo sniffed around.

"Why don't you head to the clearing?" I said. "Draven, Lien…"

They let go of one another and turned toward me.

"Take Roderick with you?" I asked.

Draven nodded and Lien frowned.

"Why aren't you coming with us?" she asked.

"I'm not going anywhere you're not," Roderick said. He swallowed, his stone neck bobbing. "It was foolish of me to split up with you during the game."

"Nonsense," I said. "I'm safe here." I locked eyes with Lien. "I just need a word with Roan, okay?"

"Come, child." Qarinah, perhaps overhearing our conversation, came up behind Roderick and put her hands on his stone shoulders.

Draven did the same to Lien. "Leave Dahlia with Sherriff Roan. He is like a father to her."

Lien frowned but turned to Draven, her hand reaching out and gripping on to Broomhelen, who must have been flying above. "I'm doing another barrier check to make sure. Come with me?"

"Of course." Draven *poofed* into a bat and they were off.

Roderick wouldn't budge and I patted Broomie around my shoulders. "Go with him?" I asked her softly. He'd seen enough death during his short time of existence, and despite how grown-up he wanted to be, he was still a kid. Broomie nodded her brush head and then rammed at Roderick's stone body until he finally took Qarinah's hand and went off with her farther into the trees toward the clearing. He stared at me over his shoulder until he stepped out of view.

"Roan," I said as more of the gray wolves stepped toward the clearing and Luna Lane's nighttime sheriff turned back to survey the scene. "You don't think this was an accident?"

I hadn't forgotten he'd declared it a "crime scene" before he'd even gotten close to the body.

"That would be something, at least," he said, sighing. He walked toward the last few standing wolves, other than Inigo, who continued to sniff all around the area. "Faine. Ma'ams. I'm going to have to ask you to step back."

My vision blurred as I fought back tears, my eyelids hot and gummy. Assuming Roan was correct —and he seemed better at telling the visiting wolves apart than I was—that meant that Echo was the wolf lying there.

The more I compared him to the other brown wolves, the more I was certain he was right. Echo had been a touch larger, a bit shaggier than his mom and aunt.

And he also had been patrolling the makeshift Team Blue headquarters last I'd seen him. He'd been on guard duty, I'd surmised. No need for him to venture into the woods to attack Team Red. What had he been doing here?

The wolf I was sure now was Serafina growled, her teeth baring up at the vampire sheriff.

The other three wolves whimpered and stood between Serafina and Roan, Cinder nudging at her flank.

"You don't have to go far," Roan said, his voice

a gentle caress. "Just step aside so we can start an investigation." He chewed his lip, his incisor drawing the dark-red venom that flowed through his veins.

The wolves all made for the stone on which King had jumped and howled, Serafina never once taking her eyes off her fallen son.

Echo had always been like a fun older brother when he'd visited.

He'd seemed so *happy*, content, despite all the tension between the families and that strange story about his ex-girlfriend.

Surely, their petty squabbles, and even an irrational ex-girlfriend, couldn't have led to this?

I eyed Inigo as he continued to sniff around, wholly focused on his task. I hadn't seen the two at each other's throats—not like Serafina and Kodiak, or Serafina and King, for that matter—but wouldn't the two of them have had the most reason to dislike each other?

Then again, it was King's daughter at the center of the fight between those two.

"King found him first," I whispered to Roan, hoping Serafina wouldn't hear. Though surely, she knew based on werewolf howling that he'd been the one to alert everyone of the tragedy. "Draven, Broomie, and I came upon the two of them. King was sniffing at the body."

Roan crouched beside the fallen Echo and my

breath caught in my throat. But I crouched down with him.

"I'll take your statement," said Roan gruffly as he pulled a plastic glove out of his pocket and affixed it to his hand. He must have carried those with him everywhere. "Just as soon as I survey the scene."

My *statement?* Like I was some mere witness whose account would get included in the report and not the person he'd trusted to help him out with cases the most?

The sound of Inigo sniffing closer reminded me that Roan had little need for me now.

Roan poked at the stained fur, gently pushing it aside.

"Did a paintball pierce his skin?" I asked. I looked around. "Where's his vest and cannon?"

Roan didn't reply at first. Then a bit more blood trickled out and I realized he must have located the wound beneath all the fur. "It's not a bullet wound —paintball or otherwise. Too small for a paintball cannonball gone awry, either."

Drawn into his discovery, I leaned closer.

It was a clean, long cut. Like a knife wound, only… "There's no sign of a struggle," I said. "The cut is too clean. You would expect if someone came at him with a knife, and even if the person managed to stab him, it'd be more jagged. What could that—"

A wolf head burst over my shoulder, pushing me

to the side to get closer to Roan and take a look. Inigo.

Sighing, Roan stood up, removing the glove. "Mayor Abdel needs to know." He checked his watch as Inigo sniffed at Echo's wound. "I only have a couple more hours. Dahlia, if I don't get your statement, stop by the office in the morning and speak to Inigo." He looked up. "I need to take Draven's statement before he heads into his coffin, too." He patted the wolf beside him. "Watch the body. Let me confer with the mayor."

Inigo sat up straight on his two back legs, the perfect police dog, only with shaggier fur than most.

"Let me help," I said, walking after Roan as he headed toward Serafina and the others. I didn't even know *why* I'd said it.

This wasn't my job.

And I'd had more than my fill of death in Luna Lane as of late.

Roan was too kind to tell me that bluntly. "Take care of Faine and her family," he said, nodding at the wolves gathered around the stone. "And get some rest, Lia. You look tired."

I did?

"You've been through a lot," he emphasized, then he turned and spoke to the wolves, informing them of his plans to speak with the mayor. I tuned out most of what he had to say.

I frowned. I had been through a lot. But so had everyone in Luna Lane.

My eyes caught Faine's. I'd never seen a wolf cry before. The tears filling her dark eyes glistened.

I wouldn't rest until I knew who'd killed her big-brother-like cousin. Even if I didn't have a badge.

There had to be *something* Roan and Inigo could use my help with.

Chapter Nine

It was a long night, made longer by the waiting.

In the back of my mind, I could hear Ginny rambling on about everything Lazarus had missed as I sat in front of the fire, petting the sleeping wolf form of Fauna, who'd curled up on the couch in Faine and Grady's house beside me. Broomie and Roderick sat in the armchair perpendicular to me, the other wolf kids curled up on the rug at our feet. Grady and Faine were with Faine's family, most of Grady's family in their wolf forms at Draven's next door.

"I never even saw the poor thing slip into the woods!" Ginny shouted, causing Fauna's ear to twitch. I pet her some more to lull her back to sleep. "At one point, he poked his head out, but then he went back behind that dreadful little shack"—she shuddered, and I remembered her own death taking place in a sort of mobile shack, albeit one supposedly better made than our wargame headquarters— "I *thought* to watch for any enemy sneaking up on us from behind. But that must have been when he skittered off. I kept my eye on the treeline in front of me. Didn't know anything was wrong until that terrible wolf howl." She shuddered again.

Lazarus stood, adjusting the cravat over his skeletal form, and somehow, with his wheezy, not quite-living-sounding voice, said, "It is a sad, sad thing. But death, my darling, is just a new journey. You know better than anyone, that if the poor young man has any regrets, and if his will is strong enough, his heart good enough—"

Ginny's ghostly eyes widened. "We'll have a new resident! Another ghost!" She slipped her spectral arm through Lazarus's bony one as they made their way to the front door. "Do you think he'll come back as a *wolf*, though? Would he be able to change?"

Lazarus patted the hand that rested on his arm. "That would be something up to him entirely. It may be, he has no regrets here, at least none that staying in Luna Lane could ever hope to make better."

"Not even pointing us to his killer?" I whispered just as they walked behind the couch.

A chill hit the air as they both stopped near me.

Fauna shivered in her sleep, not even her wolf fur enough to keep the undead's chill away.

"It wasn't an *accident*?" whispered Ginny, still a touch too loud. Though it was clear she was trying to be quiet for the kids' sake.

Roderick hung on to every word, though he kept quiet, reminding me of his silent self from only a few weeks back.

I just shook my head.

Lazarus let out a wheezing sigh. "Well, if only it were so simple, a ghost telling us the solution to their mystery." He directed his empty eye sockets toward Ginny, and her face darkened even in the ghostly afterimage that made up her form.

"It's not so easy as all that," she explained. "No, I don't think you'll find he comes back as a ghost to point out a perpetrator—it's regret about *love* that draws a soul back." She let out a loving sigh and leaned against Lazarus. "That's what I believe anyway. Not having experienced love like this— that's what drew me back."

"Oh, Virginia, you are sweet." Lazarus patted her hand again and quickly nodded my way. "Alas, I have tarried too long here. The mayor and Roan will have arranged for the poor man's body to be brought to my funeral parlor." His teeth chattered a moment. "I've never had a werewolf pass through my doors. Will he stay a wolf come sunrise? We shall have to see."

"Something even Lazarus doesn't know!" said

Ginny. She turned to me. "Grieve your werewolf friend. It is sad when one's time on Earth is cut short. But you know better than many how the realm beyond, a place of happiness, will welcome him with open arms." She nodded at me as they exited out the front door, causing Flora's head to lift up from the ground, her bleary, wolf eyes blinking.

"Back to bed," I told her.

She looked around and got up, shuffling over closer to the fire, I thought. But then she laid her chin over Roderick's stony feet. Roderick's eyes widened and Broomie giggled, her bristles rustling.

At some point, the house now quiet, I must have drifted off myself, thoughts of Echo in happier times butting up against my sleepiness.

The front door opened with a *bang* and I shot up, the kids—all in human form once more—shooting up along with me, the sun streaming in through the nearest window.

Dawn already. Roan, Draven, and Qarinah would be in their coffins now.

Had Roan solved the case before he'd gone to sleep?

As I stood, Fauna joined me, rubbing her eyes.

"Let's get upstairs, kids," I said, trying to get their attention away from whoever had just walked in, clomping angry feet across the hallway. "Get dressed and brush those teeth."

"Can't you *enchant* our teeth clean?" Fauna whined.

"Hush now," I told her. "You have to learn to take care of your teeth on your own. I won't always be there to clean them."

Flora spoke to Roderick as I tried to corral the other two werewolf kids, dodging one question after the other. Flora helped out by taking her sister's hand and leading her up in front of Falcon and me.

"Where's Mommy?" Falcon asked for the fifth time as we reached the top of the stairs, the girls' eyes trying to peer around me to get a look at whoever was making so much noise in the kitchen below.

"She'll be back soon," I said, and I made sure each got back to their rooms.

Luckily, my promise wasn't empty as Faine charged up the stairs just then, Grady right behind her. Both had puffy bags under their bloodshot eyes and clearly hadn't slept a wink.

"Thank you, Dahlia," said Faine, and I grabbed for her arm as she went to pass me and head for Falcon's room.

"Do they know who…?" I let the question go unfinished as Grady nodded curtly in acknowledgement and headed for their son's room instead to help him get ready for the day.

Faine's eyes welled up with tears. "No." She wiped some away. "Roan had to get back to his coffin. Inigo and the mayor are working out the next few steps."

"Inigo didn't get any sleep." I wasn't entirely

sure Mayor Abdel needed any. But I also knew he wasn't much of an investigator himself. He wouldn't be much help.

The door to Fauna's room opened. "Mama?"

Faine sniffled and wiped away her tears with the heel of a hand. "I'm coming, honey." She smiled, but it didn't quite reach her eyes. "Let's see what outfit you picked out for today."

I squeezed her arm and she smiled, a touch more genuinely, and left, shutting Fauna's door behind her.

I headed downstairs. Fatigue pushed like pressure at the back of my eyes, and I'd even managed to get some sleep. "YGRENE." I waved my hands over my body, giving myself a boost. For good measure, I added another "NAELC," though I'd used enchantments to clean myself and the kids last night. That must have been where Fauna had gotten the idea about me cleaning her teeth.

Roderick met me at the bottom of the stairs, Broomie wrapped around his shoulders.

"I want to go to school today," he said quietly.

My foot hovered over the last step. I'd figured he'd push himself and want to guard me all day.

"All right," I said. "If you think you're up for it. I don't know if the werewolf kids—"

"They're going," Roderick said. He straightened his back. "At least Flora is. And she promised to show her cousins the schoolhouse today."

I bit my lip. I didn't want to point out I doubted

the cousins would be going out touring a school-house, either. I doubted Nyko would have wanted to do so even before the events of last night.

"You *know* he did it!"

My attention was drawn back to the kitchen. I put a hand on Roderick's shoulder and nudged him toward the door. "We'll get going in just a minute," I whispered.

I tiptoed down the hall and peered into the kitchen.

Jonathan, Frieda, Cinder, and Serafina were all standing around. Cinder held a cup of coffee, and they all looked disheveled, their hair wild, untamed messes, their eyes as bloodshot and heavy as Grady's and Faine's.

Frieda was speaking harshly under her breath to Serafina, whose expression was so tight, her lips flattened into a curl, that it was like she was still a wolf, still growling at an enemy.

She jumped back. "You know as well as I do that a real death in a wargame comes with *conse-quences*! Accident or not! And he must *pay*."

She turned on her heel and stormed past down the hall, her gaze flicking to me wild enough to cause me to shirk back as she pounded up the stairs.

Cinder let out a dejected sigh and put her coffee cup down on the counter before following after her.

Jonathan and Frieda finally noticed me.

"Good morning, Dahlia." Frieda attempted a smile.

"Morning, Dahlia," Jonathan echoed gruffly.

Faine's mother gazed at her father. "I don't suppose you think we should get Hungry Like a Pup up and running?"

"You're not going to work today, are you?" I asked. "Luna Lane will understand if it's closed for a bit—"

"No, we better." Johnathan patted his wife's arm. "We better… We better stick to a routine. Do us good."

"Yes, I agree." Frieda wrung her hands. "Excuse me."

"But—" I started as Frieda passed by and headed upstairs. There was a guest room up there, and I knew Faine and Grady had given their room to her parents for the duration of their stay.

They wanted to work. Roderick wanted to go to school. At least in Roderick's case, he'd barely known Echo at all, though I still would have figured he could use the day off.

If I had anything to take the day off *from*, I certainly would have.

"Jonathan, you can stay closed. Really. First Taste will be open with the daytime shift, so people will have someplace to get some food if they absolutely need to."

"Food provided by Hungry Like a Pup," Jonathan pointed out. "They might run out soon. No, we'll head over there. Not much good we can do here, what with Serafina so focused on her vendetta."

I slipped inside the kitchen, lowering my voice. Though judging from the pounding up above, that was likely to be Serafina pacing. It didn't have the rapturous joy or pitter-patter sound of a child running around.

"Vendetta? Who does she think did it?"

Jonathan frowned and helped himself to the coffee Cinder had left behind, downing it all in one gulp.

"Serafina is grieving," is all he said after a minute.

"And she thinks Kodiak did it?" I prodded again. That *was* whom she'd been fighting with the other day.

"King," he said flatly.

I supposed he was the perfect suspect right now, too. Draven and I had stumbled on him alone with Echo's body, no other creature in sight.

But then again, would the killer have stuck around?

Unless…

"She thinks it was an accident?" I wasn't sure how that would track with such a clean wound, one clearly not caused by supercharged paintball ammunition. But it made more sense that the perpetrator would stick around and call for help afterward—*if* that was what King had been doing.

Jonathan grunted. "She hasn't *said* so, but I'm sure she thinks it was no accident. She's just covering her bases by saying that whether or not King meant to kill Echo, the werewolf village considers it a heinous act against the pack, particularly during a wargame."

I imagined it'd be considered a terrible act in any circumstances. But a *heinous* one? That covered intentional murder. Perhaps some form of careless manslaughter, too.

"What will happen to him? *If* he did it?" I swallowed and thought about it. "You know, he ambushed me and Broomie not too long before that. If he did it, he'd have had to have been fast…" Or maybe Echo had been lying there a while. I didn't voice that thought out loud, though.

"King claims he stumbled onto the body. That Echo was already dead when he found him."

"Oh." I crossed my arms. "But Serafina doesn't believe him."

"Nope." He set his coffee mug down and ran a hand through his hair. "And, Dahlia, you asked… Well, like with any place, any accidental killings get looked at closer in our village. The punishment, if there is to be any, depends on the circumstances."

"Except during the wargames…?" I prompted.

He nodded gruffly. "Now, this is the case for wargames that take place on village land. I've never heard of any away games leading to anyone's death before."

I blinked rapidly. That sounded as if the

wargames *within* the village most certainly *had* led to deaths at some point.

"But if this *had* happened in the werewolf village?" I asked.

"The punishment is death. Blood for blood. Death for death."

Chapter Ten

_V_esper patted Falcon's back as he followed his sisters and Roderick into the schoolhouse.

Roderick had been right about the kids' cousins, after all. Turned out all of the parents seemed to think the kids could use a distraction rather than a rest, just like Frieda and Jonathan. I figured it was more that the werewolves were in a tense place right now, and they wanted their kids safely out of the line of fire.

Broomie waved at Vesper, a dryad who didn't often leave the schoolhouse grounds. She slept by merging into the wooden walls at night, even. She'd been born of a tree planted here, and she felt as if the schoolhouse were her grotto. She'd been here decades before I had and had been my own teacher. Despite willingly never setting foot much more than a short distance outside of her grotto, she absorbed information like a tree root absorbed moisture. She knew so much about the world and taught Luna Lane's kids to prepare for it.

Vesper, all light-brown oak with leafy greens comprising her dress and long hair, even in the winter months, waved a tree-branch-like arm back at us.

Nyko watched Vesper from behind her back and scoffed, his lip curling as he stuck his face in his phone. Milah watched her more warily, even jumping back as a skittish dog might have when Vesper turned back around to follow the kids inside.

"Well, I guess we should head to the sheriff's office," I told Broomie. "Roan *did* say he'd want my statement. Maybe Inigo's ready to take it."

Broomie floated beside my head and nodded, her bristles making a sort of "uh-huh" sound that made me think she was on to me.

I really just wanted to poke around and see what anyone had learned about the incident since last night.

King seemed too obvious a suspect, being the first to stumble on the scene. There was bad blood between Kodiak and Serafina—and Echo, too—but it wasn't like I could picture any of Grady's family being capable of murder.

There was a *chance* it had been accidental somehow, and the perpetrator had panicked and fled. Understandable to a point, especially since apparently, accidental killing didn't make a difference when it came to the punishment, according to were-wolf wargame law.

But this was Luna Lane. Our jurisdiction. And if someone hadn't meant to do it, it was better to come clean. Perhaps Mayor Abdel could protect them, offer them sanctuary.

My feet halted on the sidewalk.

But if it had been an intentional act…

Wouldn't Inigo himself be the one most suspicious?

Had Roan been aware of his new deputy's past with Echo and King's daughter?

Wouldn't putting himself at the center of this investigation make it incredibly easy to cover up his own guilt?

But no. He was Grady's brother. He wouldn't have…

My chest clenched. I didn't know who would or wouldn't have. Not really. But *someone* had.

And at the very least, Inigo investigating the death of his greatest rival certainly seemed like a conflict of interest.

And if Roan didn't realize that—or hadn't been fully aware—then I owed it to him, to this town, to keep an eye on Inigo's investigation during the day.

"There you are!" The voice came from above.

Broomie looked up before I did, before Lien had even spoke.

She came in for a landing, Broomhelen wagging her brush head as she flipped right-side up into

Lien's hand and the witch's feet touched the ground.

"How was the barrier check?" I asked.

"Everything looked fine. No sign of a witch crossing into town." A sigh of relief slipped past her lips. "Can this *really* have nothing to do with the royal witches after your life? *Our* lives?"

"You weren't here last fall. Things have been happening in Luna Lane lately that make me wonder if there's such a thing as a small-town murder curse."

Lien chuckled, but the smile on her face dropped when she saw how serious I was.

She slipped beside me as I picked up my feet, headed toward the sheriff's office. "Sorry your Valentine's Day got ruined."

I thought suddenly of how I'd left my smartphone and tablet at home again last night. I hadn't even thought to go home to get them. Cable would have at least texted, and he was probably worrying about me. But he'd have to understand. Maybe he'd text Faine after a while when I didn't answer and find out I was okay—but that someone else most certainly wasn't.

"Oh, he said he'll make it up to me later. This was more important." Still, the grin that lit up her eyes made me quite aware of where her thoughts lay.

"Have you ever… dated before?" I asked her. I knew she was more my mom's age, or somewhere between Eithne and my mom. Which would have made her at least fifty, despite her youthful appearance.

"No." Her face fell. "Mother didn't condone such things. She said if I wanted a daughter, I'd have to pick a man and *end* him after 'the deed was done,' so that kind of put me off of the idea of dating. Not to mention how verboten the possibility of having a son instead was among the witches." She shuddered.

"Your father…?"

"Yeah. Never met him. Some normie man, like all witch fathers. Though I do know he was most likely of Vietnamese descent living in China. That's why Mother 'honored' him with my name."

I wondered if the "normie" aspect was a prerequisite. Vampires couldn't father children, outside of turning normies into vampires, but what if a witch dated a werewolf? Or some other paranormal creature capable of having kids?

Oh. Well, my own mother had had a kid with a gargoyle and I'd still turned out to be a witch. In fact, I'd been born with a little something extra, considering I could turn into stone and now even fly if I focused hard enough.

Maybe other witches didn't like the idea of witches with a little extra something. They certainly didn't like *me*.

"Awful," I said. What else did one say to that?

"I know you haven't met your father, either, though I know the reasons why are much different."

That was true. I wondered if… someday… I might find mine out there.

"Well, I'm happy you're finally opening yourself up." I nudged her arm. "And you're good for Draven. He's been in a bad place for a while."

"You mean because he was in love with you?"

I winced.

But she laughed. "I know all about it. It's fine. I know how important you are to him, but I think he finally understands that you and he are meant to be very good friends."

"I… I think so, too. I like that idea." And maybe if he finally viewed me the same way, we could focus on our friendship without any awkwardness between us.

"I feel so sorry for the werewolves," Lien told me, changing the subject.

"I know. I knew Echo growing up. He was a good guy." I sighed. "I can't see why anyone would want to kill him, even if they argued."

"But *someone* did. Accidentally or on purpose. Unless you think he did it to himself?"

"I don't see how." I thought about it. He'd torn off his vest somewhere and bumped into a blade in one, clean cut? No, it didn't seem likely. "I don't like to think it could be any of these werewolves—they're all friends or family of Grady and Faine— but the only ones I know for sure it couldn't have been are Faine, Grady, and their kids. I'd trust them with my life."

"I see." Lien nodded. She wasn't going to argue with me, tell me danger lurked around every corner and that I shouldn't be so trusting?

Being with Draven really *had* changed her.

"And of course, I grew up around Frieda and Jonathan, too. I can't picture them doing that. They loved Echo like a second son. Serafina, of course, wouldn't do that. Cinder—well, I don't know her well, but she loved him. She loves Serafina. Right?"

"I'd assume so if they got married." Lien cocked her head as the section of town with the town hall and the sheriff's office came into view up ahead. "But that still leaves most of the Vadases. And that big King fellow."

"True. I don't like to think anyone important to Grady could be a murderer... But I've only met them once or twice before this. Not sure I ever met King before at all."

"And he was the one you found, alone, with the body," Lien pointed out.

"Yes, but..." Did I tell her about my worries over Inigo? The old Lien would have gladly pounced on *any* reason to mistrust anyone, and if Inigo was going to be a permanent addition to Luna Lane... I had to make sure he wasn't guilty. "Speaking of that, I need to give my official statement. Was there anything you saw or heard last night that would be worth telling?" I chewed my lip as we stopped just a few feet away from the sheriff's office. "Why *were* you and Draven split up? I would have figured you'd have stuck together like glue all night. Especially since all the couples got paired on teams together. Bit of a weird coincidence, don't you think? Was it…" My voice grew hushed at the realization. "Was it related to the crime?"

Broomhelen shook her fur-like bristles in an evident bout of laughter and Broomie joined in, though whether or not she got the joke, I couldn't say.

Lien's cheeks darkened just a bit and she read-justed the orange, conical hat upon her head. "No. I, uh… Don't get mad, okay?"

"Why would I get mad…?" My brow arched.

"I cast an enchantment on the slips they were using to pick teams. Couples together, first and fore-most." She tugged on her hat's brim a little, covering her eyes. "I thought it would just be a fun little bonus for Valentine's Day. I never imagined it might wind up looking weird after a crime."

"Well, that's a relief," I said. "I was worried it might be a sign that other witches were at play here." I chuckled as Lien did not seem relieved to have admitted her meddling. "Yet even after all your efforts to make this a Valentine's Day date, you and Draven did split up at some point during the game."

"We're not *that* attached. We're not together now, are we?"

"Only because he's sleeping—something I bet

you could stand to do yourself, if you've been checking the barrier all night."

Broomhelen nudged Lien's hat and she sighed.

"Yeah, I guess I will get a bit of shut eye." She yawned. "No one's asked me to make a statement. I'm not sure I'd have much to add. I was the only non-werewolf guarding Team Red's flag. We drew lots and Draven was on the attacking team. That's all."

"Lots, huh? You didn't cast an enchantment on those?"

"No…" She winced. "Too many witnesses that time."

So she would have if there hadn't been witnesses? She was certainly in those early puppy love days.

"Who was in charge of your team?"

Lien frowned. "Well, the werewolves were doing their own thing. One of the big, brown ones seemed to be issuing orders. Those of us not werewolves on the team just decided we'd split up and help. It was Goldie's idea to draw lots to determine which direction we should all go in."

"And just one of you was going to stay with the flag?"

"Yes. All three of the little wolves were there, and one of the medium-sized brown ones. I *think* it was Faine."

I supposed I could ask Faine myself to confirm, but that seemed to track. I was certain the big, brown wolf in charge had been Jonathan, too, based on what I'd observed earlier in the evening.

"Did you leave the makeshift headquarters at any point during the night?" I asked. I'd never infiltrated that far into the woods, hadn't seen it outside of the quick walkthrough we'd all done before the game had begun.

"Nope. And I only ever took one person out of the game, too. Qarinah and Roan got a bit too close for comfort, so I climbed up onto the roof and got Roan. Qarinah was coming up around the side and I think one of the kids was trying to get her—there was a lot of fire from the back of the hut—but she was dodging and just as the vampire was about to grab the flag, Roan cheering her on all the while, we all froze. That soulful, wounded cry."

So that put Roan, Qarinah, Lien, Faine, and Faine's kids all in one place, away from the body, right before the crime. Not that I'd ever have doubted any of them.

And there had to have been a number of participants who'd been tagged out of the game gathered in the clearing by then, too. Like Nyko, Goldie, and Arjun.

Then again, I wasn't sure *when* Echo had been attacked. All I knew was he'd been alive and headed behind Team Blue's headquarters at the start of the game. He could have come into the woods at any point after that. Ginny had admitted she hadn't noticed when he'd left.

"The werewolves seemed to get what that sound meant right away," Lien continued. "The bigger one with me barked at the kids and the kids seemed eager to follow but stayed behind after being barked at one more time. A gray wolf joined us and corralled the kids a bit better, but by then, we'd all headed in the direction of the cry—Roan racing there even before I had time to think about it." She cringed. "I should have been readier, at the thought of *anyone* in danger, but I hadn't sensed the barrier around the town being disturbed, so my protective instincts hadn't kicked in. I didn't really understand what was going on."

Lien was new to any purpose besides protecting me from our wicked royal family. I knew why her first instinct had been to check to make sure no witch had crossed into town.

"Before then, did you see or hear anything… suspicious?" I asked her. "Did Echo ever get as far as the Team Red headquarters?"

Broomie floated down at that moment, settling into my hand. She stretched her shaft, shaking her head toward the sheriff's office, as if to urge me to hurry up. I patted her and ignored her—I needed to finish this discussion—and she sighed.

Lien frowned. "No, I mean—it was a game. There were sneak attacks. A gray wolf came at us a while before Roan and Qarinah did, but I couldn't say who. No other brown wolves appeared. At least none that I noticed."

"Which gray wolf?" I asked.

Lien shrugged. "I don't know. It was a pincer attack, I think. There was movement in the foliage on the other side of the shack, but I only caught a glimpse of one gray wolf on the side I was closer to."

"Was it large?" I asked. "Small?"

"I didn't get a *very* good look," Lien said. "I sent paintballs flying in that direction, but I don't think I hit them. They retreated."

"I'm just wondering if the wolf you saw was King or Kodiak or maybe even—"

The door to the sheriff's office swung open and Inigo, dressed fully in a sheriff's outfit to match Roan's, crossed his arms and leaned against the door frame.

"Inigo," he said, speaking his own name, and it took me a moment to realize he was finishing my question. How long had he been there? Had he cracked the door, listened to our conversation?

Broomie rolled her brush head.

Oh. She'd been trying to tell me something earlier.

"I was the gray wolf she shot at," he said simply. "Now, Miss Poplar, if you'd be so kind as to step inside and let me take your statement."

Chapter Eleven

"Oh. Do you need me for anything?" Lien asked, worrying her hands. She looked between Inigo and me, as if sensing some kind of tension between us.

Not *that* kind of tension. Unease, I'd say. A slight mistrust.

My eyes focused on the sheriff badge on his shirt. I was supposed to just *be okay* with a new deputy in town after having only Roan to rely on for all of my life?

"No, Miss Poplar—Lien Poplar, that is. If Sheriff Birch or I need anything from you, we'll be in touch. But Sherriff Birch specifically asked me to take Miss Poplar—Dahlia Poplar's statement."

"Just 'Dahlia' is fine," I said, my head spinning at all the gymnastics he'd had to go through to address two cousins with the same last name. Currently, I'd have the same issue with the Vadas family being in town, if I'd cared to call him "Mr. Vadas."

Inigo nodded, not saying anything, and stepped back inside. Broomhelen and Broomie did a little clump-bump, where they touched two clumps of bristles together, and Lien got ready to fly. "I'll be taking a nap," she said. "Come get me if there's even a *hint* of witches."

I hoped that wouldn't be the case, but I promised to do so.

Just the fact that Lien was so much more relaxed than she usually was—despite the *murder* in town—made me quite sure this was unrelated.

What use would witches have in coming so close to me in the woods and taking out Echo and *not* me? It wasn't like we'd be easy to mix up. I wasn't furry, and I didn't crawl around on all fours.

The sheriff's office was as small as it had ever been, but somehow, it felt more cramped when I was shuffling inside after a virtual stranger. There was the front desk—never attended—and then there was Sheriff Roan's desk a few paces behind that. The town's single jail cell hugged the wall, the door wide open. The cot inside was neatly made, and Broomie took off from my hand almost immediately to settle down all curled up on the pillow.

Inigo stopped behind Roan's desk and watched as my broomstick willingly ventured inside the jail cell but said nothing.

He sat down in Roan's tall-backed office chair, the leather worn in patches along the edges.

I looked around as I took the seat beside him. There was another desk in the corner he could have commandeered into his own. Though it was missing a computer… I supposed there hadn't been time to get him set up elsewhere.

Inigo typed a few things on the computer's keyboard and then cleared his throat. "When did you discover the scene?"

Right to it, then.

"I don't know what time it was. After King, and just a few moments before anyone else happened on the scene—besides Draven and Broomie, since we arrived together. King seemed to summon everyone else."

Inigo picked up a pen and pointed it in the direction of the cell. "And Broomie is…?"

"Broomhilde. My companion broomstick. She can back up everything I tell you."

Inigo snorted and dropped the pen on the desk, typing something up quickly.

My back stiffened. "Did I say something amusing?"

Inigo arched a brow. "No, forgive me. I just wasn't aware witches' broomsticks could speak. Not that I've met any witches other than you and Lien."

Oh. I deflated a little. "They can't speak. In words. Though they understand us all perfectly. I'm just used to people *from Luna Lane* being able to understand her, that's all."

"Well, Sheriff Birch's going to get Mr. Draven's statement tonight. If there's still any confusion, we can ask Miss Broomhilde to clarify. With an interpreter." He snorted again as he started typing.

Broomie lifted her head up off the pillow over in the cell and I shook my head at her. She watched the back of Inigo's head warily for a moment but seemed to give up, curling into a ball once more to go to sleep.

"So you would have stumbled on the crime scene sometime between 9:15 and 9:20, not too long after the time of death," Inigo said, typing.

It was my turn to ask a question. "How did *you* know what time that was? You were a wolf."

Inigo flashed me a too-quick smile. "I'm a deputy. Knowing the time of the crime is standard for most investigations. Not that you would know." He stopped typing and picked up a stack of papers, straightening them into a pile and pounding the pile on the desk. "I've been made aware that you've been consulted on previous investigations before, but am I correct to assume it's never been in any sort of *official* capacity?"

"Well, no, but——" My words came out as if sputtering and I clenched my hands over my thighs, squeezing at bundles of my skirt's fabric. "I've been really helpful. Some might say *essential.*"

"So Sheriff Birch and Mayor Amenemope tell me."

"Mayor *who?*"

"Mayor Amenemope. Your mummy mayor…?"

We stared at one another blankly.

I just realized I'd never known or at least never registered Mayor Abdel's family name before. He didn't share that name with Chione.

"You're far too formal," I finally said, crossing my arms. "You won't get far investigating in a small town if you're not friendlier."

"And amateur sleuths like you will just get in the way, small town or not." He narrowed his eyes at me.

Someone didn't want me poking around in this case.

"I told Sheriff Roan all of this. King was sniffing at the body, he howled, everyone else showed up. I didn't notice anything unusual."

"Besides the dead wolf?"

"Yes, *besides* that." I *tsked*.

"Maybe not so unusual in this town anyway." Inigo leaned back in Roan's chair, making me feel quite small in my low-back seat. "Though I'm hearing all of these murders can be traced back, in some way or another, to you."

"Not *all* of them!" I winced. "And I'll have you know, I've solved every last one."

"Still. Seems like you've been putting the whole town at risk with your presence from birth. Awful lot of good folk here, willing to get mixed up into some royal witch conflict."

"That has nothing to do with this. I think." I chewed my lip and stared down at the desk. It wasn't like I'd *asked* to be born here. It was my mom and Eithne who'd picked out the place, Mayor Abdel who'd allowed them to move here and hide me.

We were getting off-track.

"I don't know if you're implying that I had anything to do with this heinous crime, but Echo was like an older brother to me—Faine, too. *No one* from Luna Lane would have done this."

"Oh? Just like I suppose no vampire from Luna Lane was feeding on elderly citizens to the point of death, no ghost from Luna Lane was enacting her revenge on her killer and putting half the town at risk?"

That latter accusation was a *slight* exaggeration, but... "So you *do* know not every crime that's happened here had to do with me and this 'royal witch conflict,' as you called it."

Inigo leaned his elbows on the chair's armrests, steepling his fingers together and touching his lips.

"I was never alone in the woods! And I don't just mean Broomie. There were all of *seconds* between encounters with teammates and Team Red foes. I mean, maybe minutes a couple of times. I don't know. It was all so fast-paced. I didn't keep track of the time."

"I didn't say you'd need an alibi. Any reason why you feel the need to tell me you had one?" He leaned forward, putting his elbows on the table. "Or you *sort of* had one? It doesn't take long to stab a wolf—"

"I didn't do it!" I shouted.

Broomie shot up from the cot and flew back to my side.

Inigo chuckled and leaned back. "I didn't say you did."

That weaselly deputy… I wasn't used to Luna Lane's law enforcement not having my back.

Broomie curled up in my lap and I pet her, maybe a little too roughly. Her little head shook back and forth as I brushed my palm over her bristles, and if she'd had eyes, I would have pictured the lids pulling backward like they would have on a cat.

"You know, *I* have a few questions about you. As a concerned citizen."

"Oh?" Inigo leaned back and gestured for me to continue before steepling his hands together once more.

"You said you were at Team Red's headquarters at one point. I saw you with Milah after that. Had to be after Roderick took you out of the game."

"Yes. Milah did stick with me until that point, though we got separated for a bit when Mr. Mahajan started chasing her. The weakest member of the pack is always a liability."

I didn't like how dismissively he'd said that. As if Milah could help her age or size.

"Was she the other wolf in the foliage when Lien spotted you?"

"Yes. She's not quite experienced enough to make the most of a pincer maneuver. She retreated first—and that's when Mr. Mahajan spotted her. During her retreat."

"But eventually, he took you out. And you… headed back to the clearing?"

"I did," he said, but his voice was clipped.

"Alone?" I prodded.

Inigo licked his lips. "I have no alibi for the estimated time of the crime, if that's what you're asking. I was in the woods on my way to the clearing. I encountered no one after I saw Mr. Mahajan and you."

Broomie lifted her head up off of my lap as if to tell him she'd seen him then, too. He ignored her.

"You didn't hear anything strange? I thought werewolves had enhanced hearing."

"We do. I heard other wolves on the hunt. Normies and other paranormals clomping around more noisily. Whimpers and growls, but no screams or arguments. At least not as far as my *enhanced hearing* could reach."

He stared me down, as if daring me to question him.

I kept petting Broomie and she kept her head swiveled in his direction.

"So… I hear that you and Echo… had a past." There. Two could play at this game.

A smirk fell off Inigo's face. "That has nothing to do with this."

"Oh? You aren't looking for a *motive*? Sorry, I know I'm just an *amateur sleuth*, but I thought that was basic detective work?" I blinked rapidly, dazzling him with a toothy smile.

Inigo snorted and leaned back in his chair. "I don't have anything to hide."

"Then I can ask you how you felt about your girlfriend cheating on you with Echo?"

His shoulders drooped.

"Or how she was pregnant and claimed it was his, but then she left town?"

Inigo reached for the pen he'd discarded and clutched it tightly in one hand.

"Lexa Bane was the one who hurt me, not Echo. He didn't know she was dating anyone else, either. She told us both to keep it quiet."

I scoffed. "She sounds like a real peach."

The pen snapped. "You don't know a thing about her."

Neither did you, apparently, I wanted to say. But I bit my tongue. The feeling of euphoria that had washed over me as I'd watched him crack was like a jagged knife to the heart now as I saw the droop in his shoulders, the tremble in his hand, still clutching the broken pen.

I tried another tack and cleared my throat.

"So why did you both like her? Echo never seemed like the type to settle down. I suppose she must have… on the surface… seemed like quite a catch."

Sighing, Inigo leaned back in his chair, letting the pen go and ignoring the blue ink stain on his palm. "She was sweet. Her smile was enough to lift the cloud hanging over every rotten day." His own smile seemed pained, and it faded quickly. "She was good with kids, unlike me. Probably why she was drawn to Echo."

"He *was* good with kids. He spent the summers here growing up, mostly. But he was great with Faine, me, and our friends. We all looked up to him."

Inigo swallowed. "The kids up in the village, too. He and Nyko were especially close—once."

"Not anymore?"

Inigo shrugged. "Nyko's almost eighteen. Even older-brother types a kid once worshiped can seem like an annoyance at that age. Especially when they agree with parents."

"Petra asked Echo to say something to Nyko at some point recently?"

Inigo fluffed the air. "Yeah. Nothing important. Just normal teenage stuff. Backtalk, staying out late, that kind of thing."

"And she asked *Echo* to speak to him? Not you, her own brother?"

"Like I said. I'm not good with kids."

I wasn't sure he was good with *anyone*, but I refrained from saying that.

"So this tension between your dad and Serafina, it hasn't stopped your entire families from interacting or anything?"

"Of course not. Grady is married to Serafina's niece. It'd be too awkward to be at each other's throats *all* the time."

"And yet Echo mentioned that the fight Serafina and your father got into when they pulled up to Faine's house started in Creekdale, during a rest stop."

Inigo nodded curtly. "Earlier on the drive, there was a time when Dad had to slam on the brakes. Animal in the road. Serafina was behind us and her car nudged ours—just a little. Dad had wanted to get out then, but Mom convinced him to keep going. At the gas station, he inspected the damage. The van needs a new fender, but it's not a big deal. It runs just fine."

I hadn't noticed that.

"Was Serafina's car damaged?"

"Just a scratch. But they take any excuse to let their old rivalry over land borders heat up. They got into a fight about who owed whom. Serafina blamed my dad for that sudden stop. Dad said it was either that or hit the animal."

"What kind of animal?"

Inigo's eyebrows darted up halfway to his hairline. "Is there a point to these questions?"

I shrugged. "Just wondering how two families that are supposed to *mostly* get along could wind up in a situation where one family member winds up dead."

A long breath escaped Inigo's lips as he stood. "I was asleep when it shot across the road. Woke up as Dad was slamming on the brakes, but I saw the tail end of something heading into the woods. Probably a coyote. Didn't think it important to ask. Wouldn't make much of a difference when it came to who owes whom. Serafina was following too closely."

I stood too. "I see… I take it we're done here?"

Inigo gestured for the door. "You can see yourself out. If I need you, I'll be in touch."

"I'm sure you will." I waited for Broomie to finish stretching midair and land back in my hand, brush head up.

But I'll try keeping tabs on what you're up to today, and I'll tell Roan everything I learn as soon as he wakes up.

Chapter Twelve

I didn't get far outside of the sheriff's office before the doors to the town hall opened and out stepped Chione and Mayor Abdel.

"Dahlia," said the mummy mayor, lifting a bandaged hand as he moved down the steps toward me. "Just the witch I hoped to see. Have lunch with us?"

"Sure?" I asked, looking to Chione for explanation. It would be more like brunch, since it was still around ten in the morning. She nodded grimly, her multiple, small, dark braids swinging in the air just a little. They were both dressed in sleek suits—the mayor's a navy blue that drew out the dingy white of the magic bandages that kept him alive, Chione's a bright yellow that popped against her dark complexion—and it made Chione in particular look elegant, with her long, lanky limbs. Chione's breath turned to mist in the air, though

Mayor Abdel, I assumed, didn't breathe and didn't seem at all affected by his choice not to wear a jacket.

"MRAW," I said as Chione joined us on the sidewalk, waving my free hand over her.

She smiled. "Thank you."

Mayor Abdel stared at his granddaughter for a moment. "Where's your coat?"

She rolled her eyes. "I haven't worn one all day. You're just now noticing?"

Mayor Abdel frowned, his dark lips exposed behind the bandages, as were his large, brown eyes. "You must remind me of normie things like this, granddaughter. You know I have a lot on my mind."

"I know. I'm your personal assistant." She stuck her nose in the air just a bit, and I didn't feel there was any tension between the two of them. Chione had always seemed too proud to ask for help—and proud to be working so closely with the living paranormal ancestor in her family.

"Hungry Like a Pup is supposed to be open," I said, though I still didn't get why Jonathan and Frieda would open it on a day like today.

"I was thinking more First Taste," said the mayor, and before I could ask if it was a good idea to be drinking during the day, he turned and led the way.

"It's been a long night," Chione told me as she stepped beside me, on the side where I was holding Broomie, brush head upright. Broomie waved at

Chione, who smiled and nodded at her. "Good morning, Broomhilde."

"Did you get any sleep last night?" I asked Chione, my voice a whisper. Mayor Abdel was a few paces ahead of us. Chione usually chauffeured him around town, but the pub wasn't too far away.

"No," she said softly. "He will order alcohol—but I will order coffee." She yawned. "Neither one affects my grandfather regardless, but he does so enjoy the taste."

"I can enchant you some extra energy," I offered.

Chione let out a sigh. "Please."

"YGRENE," I said, waving a hand over her again.

The bags under her eyes smoothed out just a bit, and Chione got a spring in her step, her wedge heel hitting the sidewalk with more force.

"What was that?" Mayor Abdel turned around to look at us.

"Nothing, Grandfather," Chione said, again proving my theory that she didn't like to speak up to her paranormal relative about any normie discomfort she might be experiencing.

She didn't need to pretend to be so strong—she *already* was plenty strong, in my opinion.

When we entered First Taste, a blast of warm air met my face, and Broomie and I both let out a sigh of relief at once. I hadn't renewed my own warmth enchantment in some time.

The thunder sound effect rolled out into the pub and Mayor Abdel went straight for town hall's favorite booth at the back. On the wall above him was a painting of a castle in Transylvania, complete with the depiction of a dark and stormy night.

"The usual for me," said Mayor Abdel as he lifted a hand and caught Jamie's attention. The gangly young man with golden-brown hair that curled down over his bronzed complexion looked up from wiping a glass and nodded at the town's mayor.

Chione kept walking toward the door at the back, which connected to Hungry Like a Pup. "None for me, thanks," she said to the normie dayshift bartender. "I will get some coffee."

"Dahlia?" Jamie asked. I stood halfway to the table the mayor had selected, my feet rooted to the ground at the sight of the only other customer here so early in the morning.

King Bane was sitting alone at the counter, throwing back, judging from the empty shot glasses next to him, his third hard drink.

"Oh, sparkling water, please," I said.

King turned and eyed me as I spoke, his gaze landing pointedly on Broomie. Broomie slipped out of my grip and floated across the pub to join Mayor Abdel, sitting upward in imitation of a human with her shaft curled beneath her on the booth seat.

King held his shot glass between his fingers and locked eyes with me before turning back to Jamie and slamming his shot glass on the counter. "Another."

Jamie frowned. "I'm not sure that's a good idea."

King pounded the table with two of his fingers. "Keep 'em coming."

Jamie turned to me, as if *I* had any say in how much the man drank, and spun around to grab a bottle of amber-colored liquor. I was sure Draven and Qarinah had a policy for anyone who seemed to be drinking too much—Draven had certainly tried to stop *my* drinking and I'd barely had anything—but I knew Jamie to be a bit of a pushover.

I slipped into the booth beside Broomie, leaving room for Chione to slide in beside me when she got back, and taking up position to observe King.

"What can I do for you, Mayor?" I asked, threading my fingers together in front of me and focusing on King instead of the man to whom I was speaking.

"Ah, yes," he said, as Jamie came over with a mug of frothy beer and a glass of sparkling water. "I wanted to hear your opinion… on our new deputy sheriff."

We thanked Jamie for the drinks and though the bartender partially blocked my view of King across the room, I was quite certain I noticed the way King stiffened at the mayor's question. Cradling a drink, he even turned his head just slightly, keeping an eye on us, too.

I swiveled to Mayor Abdel, pretending I hadn't noticed that as Jamie walked away.

"I've barely spoken to him," I admitted. "He seems… professional. Maybe a bit *too* professional. But considering what's happened here on his first day, maybe that's not a bad thing." I took a sip of my drink, my mouth suddenly quite dry, as Broomie let out a little cooing sound and her brush head drooped.

Why was the mayor asking me this?

"No one told me you were hiring a daytime deputy sheriff," I said, turning the cold glass in my hands a little.

"Yes, well, we couldn't very well have no law enforcement on call during the day, could we? Not even in Luna Lane." The mayor cleared his throat. "Though lately, perhaps I should say *especially not* in Luna Lane."

"I'd have helped Roan," I said softly. "I know I don't have formal training, but—"

Mayor Abdel held up a hand. "The prospect was floated. I'm sorry to say I preferred more experience. That's not to say you couldn't work alongside Roan and Inigo if you'd like. We may have room in the budget for part-time—"

"No, that's fine." My heart slunk a little. At least that meant Roan actually *had* considered taking me on, despite what he'd also said about Inigo having more experience. Maybe that was why he'd been reluctant to share the news with me.

I didn't really *want* to be the town's law enforcement, officially. I'd just have been willing to step up to help Sheriff Roan. I had the power to defend people, and more than a little investigative knowhow, if I did say so myself.

Broomie shot up straight as Chione appeared beside the table, sliding into the booth with a steaming paper cup and a stack of to-go containers. "I thought I'd get something to share," she said, and I focused across the room on King as she popped open the containers and slid one in front of her grandfather, then Broomie, then me, keeping one for herself. Broomie dug into a container jammed with cornhusks with gusto.

"Thank you," I said, the scent of steaming hot pancakes drawing my attention away from the older werewolf by his lonesome at the bar.

Chione passed out little containers of syrup to everyone but Broomie—who probably wouldn't appreciate the sticky mess on her dried cornhusks.

I picked up the plastic cutlery in the waxy box beside the pancakes. "What do you two think of Inigo?" I asked.

King turned his head just slightly again.

"Professional, just like you said," Mayor Abdel added. "Though he was a wolf over night, I was surprised he was still so vigilant and helpful with the investigation."

"He and Roan seemed able to communicate, more or less," added Chione, taking a sip of her coffee. "Excellent teamwork. And besides, he'll be a wolf only once a month. And nights are when he'll typically be off shift—unless an emergency pops up again."

"Oh, yes, I can't fault him for being a werewolf. In fact, his talents were quite useful," Mayor Abdel added, chewing a bite of pancake rather loudly. He didn't need to eat, but he did anyway.

Same with Broomie, who leaned back in the booth and made a sound with her bristles that sounded halfway between a quack and a burp.

"What do you mean?" I asked. "How did his 'wolf talents' come in handy last night?"

"He found a trail," said Chione, cutting into her pancake stack. "From the Team Blue wargame headquarters to where the body was found. The wolf's exact path before his death. It's all been marked for further investigation during the day."

Mayor Abdel nodded, cutting his own pancakes up into smaller pieces. I wondered if they ought to even be sharing this information with me, an *amateur* investigator, but we were such a small-knit town, and I was usually let in on such investigations, I suppose they didn't even think twice about it.

"I was wondering if you might consider assisting Inigo today?" Mayor Abdel asked before popping more pancake into his mouth. "Show him around town? Introduce him to the people, in Roan's stead?"

My own pancake felt heavy on my fork. Was *that* why he'd asked me my opinion on the man?

"I don't think he'd appreciate that," I told him honestly. "I didn't exactly make a great impression during my statement this morning."

Across the bar, King was standing, pulling a wallet out of his pocket.

"Nonsense," said Mayor Abdel, chewing loudly again. One of his bandages at his ear flopped with the movement of his jaw. He leaned closer to me. "And frankly, though I have every faith this tragedy will be resolved quickly, I'd prefer to keep a trustworthy eye on the situation. Just until we're sure he's one of us." He straightened up and cut into his pancakes again. "I'm sure he'd be grateful for any help your enchantments can provide."

"Well, maybe," I said, my eyes still on King as he and Jamie settled his tab. I looked to Chione. "Can you excuse me? I need the powder room."

Chione slid out of the booth as I stuffed my mouth full of pancake in case what I actually had in mind took longer than I thought. Broomie followed me out and slid into my hand just as I intentionally-*unintentionally* bumped into King headed, I found, not to the front door but toward the door connecting to Hungry Like a Pup.

"Excuse me," I said, laughing, though the sound of the forced laughter was hollow even to my ears.

King eyed me up and down and grunted, about to move on his way.

"I'm surprised to find you in town," I said, stopping him in his tracks. "So early in the day, I mean."

"Nothing else to do. If it were up to me, I'd have left at dawn. But I can't exactly leave during an ongoing murder investigation that's pegged me as a suspect, can I?"

My eyelids fluttered rapidly. I hadn't expected him to be so blunt about it. I also hadn't gotten the impression from Inigo that King was the prime suspect, even considering he'd been found first with the body and his history of sorts with the victim.

Maybe Inigo played it close to the vest.

Jamie, who was in the midst of picking up King's empty glasses a few feet away, stared brazenly in our direction.

"I'd like to hear your side of the story," I said. He opened his mouth, but before he could say anything, I pointed over my shoulder. "Our mayor asked me to assist the sheriff's office in this investigation." I leaned closer conspiratorially. "As I think you heard."

King slammed his mouth shut and crossed his arms. He seemed remarkably in control of himself despite the number of drinks he'd downed. "What do you want to know?"

So he wasn't going to fight this? *I'd better act fast before he changes his mind.*

"You attacked Team Red—in the wargame," I

said, adding the last part quickly. "I was there. Then you retreated, and a few minutes later, Draven, Broomie, and I found you sniffing Echo's body."

"I was on my way back to Team Blue's headquarters. I needed more cannonballs. I was rushing along, but then I… I smelled death." He cleared his throat.

"So you *sought out* that scent. You didn't stumble onto the path with Echo in it?"

He scoffed. "No. But I was alone. I can't prove I took a detour. What was I supposed to do, ignore that wretched scent? I'm one of the pack leaders. It could have been anyone. I can't ignore something like that."

"Did you smell anyone else in the area?"

"No one too close. But I could smell *everyone* involved in the game, other than the vampires. They don't really give off much of a scent."

Broomie nodded, as if she were capable of smelling anything. Not since she'd lived her cat lives, as far as I knew. Then again, perhaps she'd smelled a vampire when she'd been a cat.

But Draven, Roan, and Qarinah all had alibis, and besides, I wouldn't doubt a single one of them. They had no motive regardless.

"What about Echo's cannon and vest? Did you see them?"

"No." King narrowed his eyes. "I wasn't exactly looking for those. More focused on the dead member of my pack."

"Yes, but… You and Echo…" I swallowed, and my gaze flicked over to Mayor Abdel and Chione. I found them both staring in our direction, so I leaned over and spoke softer. "I know about Lexa."

King jolted. "She's got nothing to do with this."

She wasn't even here. I wasn't saying she *had* been responsible. Directly.

"Sure, but I mean… Things had to be awkward between you and Echo, right? You're the only one who knows where Lexa is, and her child is Echo's, too? He never asked you to help him get in touch with your daughter after she left?"

"She isn't his," King said abruptly. He put a hand on the swinging door leading to the restaurant next door. "And I've had enough of you butting into my business. Show me a badge or ask your questions elsewhere." He disappeared inside the restaurant.

There was a flurry of activity in my peripheral vision as Jamie started whistling a little too innocently and wiping up the counter in a single spot over and over again. So he'd been eavesdropping, too.

I wondered if I should follow after King, though not to talk. That would probably do me little good at this point.

Still, what he'd said. *"She isn't his."* At first, I'd thought he'd meant Lexa, although the phrasing would have been a touch possessive for a couple dating. Not to mention, it didn't quite work if King remembered he ought to speak about Echo in the past tense. Not that people didn't slip up like that shortly after someone's passing.

But I'd also asked about Lexa's child, the one she'd claimed had been Echo's.

She. Lexa was out there with a little girl.

And King had most definitively declared that Echo wasn't the father. Which made Inigo still being mad at Echo seem less likely, if there was some other man out there who'd fathered a child with their ex.

Maybe Inigo hadn't been lying when he'd said he blamed Lexa for the cheating more than he blamed Echo.

Broomie nudged my cheek with her bristles. I'd been lost in thought.

Did Lexa's situation have anything to do with Echo's death? If not, then, well, it wasn't my business.

If it did have something to do with her death, though, if only to serve as motivation… I needed to find out where she was and if there was any way to contact her.

Chapter Thirteen

I finished my pancakes and informed Mayor Abdel and Chione that the conversation they'd witnessed me having with King was the start of me helping Inigo with this mystery.

Only, I may have fudged the "helping Inigo" part of it. We could both look into things and come together in the end to share our findings.

Even if Inigo hadn't been so close to this case— so close that I still wasn't entirely convinced he was in the clear—I doubted he wanted to work *with* me, anyway. Since I was an amateur, after all.

By the time I'd finished brunch with the mayor and Chione, there was no sign of King next door in Hungry Like a Pup when I peered in, just Jonathan and Frieda hard at work. Not that I'd expected him to stay in there another twenty minutes.

"Do you think I should check on Faine?" I asked

Broomie as she flew us down the block. I kept my eye out for anything unusual.

Broomie nodded at first, then shook her head.

"I suppose she would be using this time without the kids and with her parents at the café to sleep," I said to my broomstick. "I don't think any of the werewolves besides the kids got a wink of sleep last night." I nudged her toward the woods, the scene of the crime. "Let's take a look at things in the light of day, and without everyone else crowding around. I bet Inigo flagged the path Echo took so Sheriff Roan could get a better look at it."

Broomie nodded, and off we flew to the edge of town.

Broomie came in for a landing by the Team Blue makeshift headquarters first at the treeline in the clearing. In the distance, there was movement on Jeremiah's farm, the farmer bringing crates out of a greenhouse to the back of his pickup truck.

The snow was sloshy in patches, paw- and foot-prints of the wolf and humanoid variety spread widely throughout the clearing, and especially around the makeshift hut. It had always been a slap-dash job, but in the daylight, after so much activity, it was starting to wear down, a plank of plywood on one side not lined up correctly and threatening to make the entire thing collapse.

"There's a little yellow flag in the snow there. I was right. I've seen those at the sheriff's office.

Those must be to mark Echo's path last night after the game started."

Broomie took us to the ground, my black boot crunching in the snow.

There was a circle of wolf pawprints behind the makeshift headquarters, the snow so worn, the mud beneath was showing in patches, like one wolf had paced here quite a few times. I peered inside the gaping hole in the plywood acting like a window of sorts and saw the Team Blue paintball ammunition and extra goggles and vests stacked inside still. Our yellow team flag still flew high behind a stack of tires, no team having been declared the winner last night.

"There are several sets of pawprints leading to this location," I told Broomie. "But only that line leading away from the back of the hut." Sure enough, there was another yellow sheriff's flag at the edge of the woods, the complete opposite direction of Team Red's headquarters deep in the woods beyond the clearing behind me. "Let's finish checking out this area, and then we'll head that way."

I knew my bootprints were only adding to the confusion at this point, but there wasn't enough room inside the makeshift headquarters to float on Broomie or spread my wings as a gargoyle. I tried to avoid transforming casually regardless, since Broomie seemed to take offense to not being my sole mode of flying transportation.

"WOLG," I said, waving a hand that started to glow. Light streamed in through the holes at the seams and windows, but there was still a lot covered in shadow. There were still a few paintball weapons left here, no one in the mood to clean up—or perhaps the investigation decreeing that everything had to be left as is. There was an extra wolf-sized vest with a paintball mini-cannon attached. "Do you think this was Echo's?" I asked Broomie.

She peered around and bobbed her bristles at it, as if sniffing it, though she had no sense of smell. Then she shook her head. It did look pristine and unused. Even if Echo had never fired a shot—which I wasn't sure had been the case yet—there would have been some wear and tear on this vest. It looked brand new, never worn.

"Probably just for backup, in case someone's vest or cannon broke," I told my broomstick.

I looked around some more, gesturing my glowing hand at everything else in the hut. There was a low, biting wind that didn't chill me thanks to my warmth enchantment, but it did mess my hair as it swept through the gap where one wall was shifting out of place.

Broomie shook wildly, and Ginny's story about how a shed's collapse had played a role in her death came immediately to mind.

"Just a second more," I told her, finishing up my sweep.

The walls were truly *creaking* now.

Broomie tugged on my arm from where she stood in my grip, and we flew out of the hut, me dangling on my broomstick by one hand.

Just in time for it to collapse right in front of us.

I let out a yell and covered my face with my free arm. A moment later, the place went quiet, and I looked up to find the tires and pieces of headquarters scattered everywhere, even the paintball ammunition rolling about the clearing.

Some distance away, a truck started up and it took me a moment to realize the truck was headed my way from Jeremiah's farm. Off road, straight down the clearing between the two parts of the woods.

"Oh, Jeremiah must have heard the collapse and my scream," I told Broomie. "Let's go meet him halfway, before his truck adds to the confusion of part of the crime scene." I slid on her back and we flew out toward the truck. "Thank you, girl," I whispered to her, leaning backward on my broomstick to speak nearer her head.

She giggled.

The truck came to a steady stop with a squeal of breaks still quite a distance from the collapsed Team Blue headquarters and Broomie lowered us to the driver's side window, which rolled down.

"Everything all right, Dahlia?" Jeremiah asked, scratching his short, blond beard. "That made an awful racket, and I heard a scream."

My voice certainly had carried on the wind.

"That was me," I said, putting my feet on the ground and flipping Broomie upside down in my hand. "Mayor Abdel asked me to help with the investigation, and I was over there, looking for clues when…" I gestured back, at the collapsed head-quarters some distance away.

"Just the two of you?" Jeremiah asked.

"Yes." I cleared my throat. "Sherriff Vadas is tackling other aspects of the investigation." *And has no idea I've been asked to assist him*, I added only in my head.

"Well, all right, then. Shame what happened at you all's little game last night." He stared ahead at the clearing in front of him.

My gaze glanced over the crates in the back. The bed of the truck was only about half full and the crates had shifted around a bit, berries and cabbage tumbling out, in Jeremiah's haste to see if anyone had needed his help.

"YDIT," I said, waving my free hand at the truck bed. Jeremiah turned around to watch as my enchantment picked up the produce that had tumbled about and put it back in its crates.

"Thank you," he said, turning off the engine of his truck and opening his door. I stepped back to allow him space. "Didn't even consider the goods when I heard that noise."

He walked around the truck to inspect it, though my enchantment had cleaned it all up. But a thought occurred to me as I watched his eyes narrow over the crates, his lips mouthing a count of the vegetables.

"Have Roan or Inigo talked to you yet?" I asked. "About last night?"

Jeremiah focused on the crates but shook his head. "All I know is what Goldie and Arjun told me this morning when I swung by Vogel's."

"Did you notice anything last night? Anything out of the ordinary? I saw smoke coming from your chimney when our game started, so I assumed you were still awake."

Jeremiah nodded and brought the tailgate of the truck bed back up, slapping his palm against the vehicle twice as if out of some habit to signal to a driver to take off with the load.

"I went to bed around ten. I could hear the wolves howling for a while before then. Good thing I'd asked one of them fellows earlier in the day what they were up to, dragging all that junk out to the clearing and the woods."

"Who'd you talk to?" I asked.

"Didn't get his name. Looked a lot like Grady, only older. Figured it was his father." Jeremiah shivered, despite the big, Sherpa-lined coat and hunter's cap he had on. I performed a warmth charm on him, and he let out a smile.

"Should have you stop by the farm again sometime, hit me with those warmth charms all winter."

I hadn't been to Jeremiah's much to help since my one-good-deed-a-day curse of sorts no longer applied. He lived alone and seemed to like working alone, only sometimes asking for help at harvest.

"Did you notice anything else strange that night? When did you know a wolf had died?"

"Like I said, not until this morning." Jeremiah leaned against his truck. "And I sleep pretty soundly. Plus, I brushed off any noise I heard as just part of the game you all were playing."

"What kinds of noises?"

He frowned. "Well, the wolf howling, for one. That was mostly off in the distance."

"'Mostly'?" I looked beyond the truck at his farmhouse some distance away. It was certainly out of bounds of any gameplay.

"Well, I did think I heard some wolf sounds a little closer to home," Jeremiah said, crossing his arms. "But I looked outside and didn't see anything."

"Howling?" I clarified.

He chewed his lip. "No, more like panting. Like a wolf tired of running."

My spine tingled. Like a killer wolf who'd fled the scene, albeit briefly, since every wolf was accounted for shortly thereafter?

Then why run in the first place?

"About what time was that?" I asked.

Jeremiah didn't hesitate. "About 9:30. I know because my evening news was winding down and I'd been about ready to get to bed."

That put this mysterious noise not too long after

the time of the crime, which Inigo had insisted had been about 9:15 to 9:20. Though everyone had been gathered around the crime scene around 9:30, I'd wager. "Did you go outside to check?"

Jeremiah shook his head. "Just checked out the window. Like I said, I assumed it had to do with the game. I've never been worried about my farm's safety in Luna Lane." He stared me down. "Though I suppose lately…"

Lately, there'd been a number of crimes in our little town.

I knew his farm was some distance away, but I wondered at Roan not having time to let him know a killer was on the loose nearby. I supposed he'd thought it better to keep an eye on all of the suspects.

"Did you find anything off when you came outside this morning?" I asked.

He shook his head. "No. I'd all but forgotten about the panting sound until you asked me just now, though. I wasn't on the lookout for anything."

"Do you mind if I have a look around?" I asked. Broomie shifted her head back in the direction of the woods. I knew I hadn't followed the path Echo had taken yet, but this seemed like a good lead to follow, too.

Jeremiah tilted his head. "You really think it might be worth checking out?"

"I do."

Just then, the sound of another vehicle—easy to

pick up in this remote corner of town—drew our attention toward Jeremiah's farm.

It was Sheriff Roan's truck, only I knew Sheriff Roan was fast asleep in his coffin in his basement.

The engine shut off as the vehicle parked in front of Jeremiah's farm, and the echo of a door opening and then slamming rung out over the clearing.

"That's Inigo," I told Jeremiah.

The farmer nodded. "Looks like he's come to ask me about last night, after all."

So Inigo was about to get the lead on Jeremiah's new clue, too.

"I suppose he could check out the farm," I said, thinking. Did I want to confront the new deputy sheriff and let him know what I was up to? I *did* have Mayor Abdel's permission—his plea for help, even.

But no. I wasn't quite ready for that yet. And I didn't want him to stop me from checking out the crime scene in the light of day. Better to ask forgiveness than permission.

"Why don't you tell him what you told me and I'll meet up with you later?" I suggested, getting on Broomie's shaft.

"Sure," said Jeremiah. "Or you can both look around."

"Don't let him know I'm out here," I said, not knowing what else to say to Jeremiah's quirked brow. It was suspicious, I got it. And frankly, if Inigo *was* hiding something, I wasn't too sure I'd find any clues at Jeremiah's farm once he was done visiting the place. I watched his figure in the distance, though. He went up to the farmhouse's front door and knocked on it. So he wasn't off to explore the farmhouse without the owner's permission and hide any clues.

Then again, maybe he was just making sure Jeremiah wasn't home to witness him in action.

"Best get back there," I said. Maybe Inigo wouldn't do anything to destroy evidence if Jeremiah was there.

But I have no concrete evidence he's even a part of this crime, I reminded myself.

"I've still got things to look for here," I said quickly, and Broomie and I took off for the woods.

Chapter Fourteen

*B*roomie and I encountered some resistance as we tried to float over the path of the flags leading into the woods so as not to disturb the path. Every so often, Broomie's bristles would snag in a twig, or she'd have to maneuver tightly between two tree trunks up ahead.

I didn't exactly want to go through the woods blasting nature out of my way with enchantments.

"Maybe I should get down," I told Broomie. "You'd have an easier time getting around without worrying about me riding."

Behind me, Broomie shook her head vigorously.

"I won't turn into a gargoyle and fly myself," I promised her. Though I really wished she would see it more as me flying *with* her, not making her obsolete. She was more than just my conveyance. I pointed to a small spot between trees to the side of the marked path. "Let's travel alongside the path so we don't disturb it."

That seemed to satisfy Broomie and she headed for the spot I'd indicated. After a bit more rigmarole sliding off of her—complete with twigs getting caught in both Broomie's bristles and my hair—I landed on my feet, looking both ways along the marked path.

So far, I hadn't noticed anything, other than the fact that wolves were able to force their way through even the densest of foliage far better than a witch on a broom.

"No human—or human-like paranormal—has come this way," I pointed out. "There'd be more disturbance to the brush, like branches snapped back above a wolf's height. That means Inigo left the flags in his wolf form." Well, that made sense. He'd been the one to sniff the path Echo had taken. "But Roan still hasn't been this way? Maybe he kept busy with other parts of the investigation before dawn."

I frowned and kept looking around. Without a wolf's sense of smell, I had no way to determine if this really was the path Echo had taken. But so far, it tracked. Echo had gone into the woods near the back of Team Blue's headquarters hut, then taken the long way around, through the woods rather than the clearing, to get over here to the trees on the other side of the clearing, approaching Team Red's headquarters somewhere up ahead.

Broomie shook her bristles and floated over the path. I was right; she had an easier time of it without me weighing her down. She pointed at a spindly twig sticking out of a barren bush.

"What's that?" I asked, leaning over a bit to peer closer. "A clump of brown fur?"

She nodded vigorously.

"Well, that helps prove Inigo was right about Echo taking this path. Unless another member of the family with brown fur also went this way." I cocked my head. "Do you think I should use an enchantment to check if the fur is his?"

Broomie folded in on herself, adjusting the tail end of her shaft under her brush head as if like a fist supporting her chin—pondering my question.

"Wait," I told her after a bit. "You're right. I don't think I know an enchantment that can do that. That's more of a potions thing. We'd better leave it. It was probably his. Let's keep going."

We did, me doing my best not to trample a path alongside the flagged one, but it was getting more and more difficult to leave the trail pristine. By the time Roan got here, he'd notice the human-sized person who'd traveled alongside the path right away —me, hours after the crime had taken place.

I sighed.

This had better prove worthwhile.

That wasn't the only clump of brown fur we found stuck on nature along the way. And there were plenty of pawprints, too, though it took me a second to realize the ones that sort of went around in circles were just slightly smaller than the ones moving straight ahead, and they often led to a flag. So those were Inigo's footsteps as he'd marked the path.

"We're still looking for Echo's vest and paintball cannon," I told Broomie. "Though I suppose if it were easily found here, I'd have a hard time believing Inigo missed it during his sweep."

We were coming up on an area I felt seemed sort of familiar. Then again, it had been dark and I'd been on the hunt for Team Red members as I'd walked this way last night, but still, there were signs of human-sized trampling up ahead, more in line with my path parallel to Echo's. There was a particularly large area of brush that seemed flattened.

"This was where I came across Nyko," I told Broomie. I pointed to the bush where she and I had hidden in order to surprise Goldie. "So Echo was…" I looked over. "He passed by? I wonder if that was before or after Nyko got taken out. I mean, I saw Echo over there, back in the clearing, then I crossed the clearing and came into the woods myself… Echo *could* have been fast enough to bolt the long way around and catch up. But why do that? Some kind of strategy to approach Team Red's headquarters?" I tapped a finger to my lips. "Unless Serafina and Cinder were aware he'd left, it seems foolish to leave the back of the headquarters unguarded like that. The perfect chance for an enemy to snatch the flag, sneak up on the guards from behind."

Broomie came over and bobbed her head in what it took me a moment to realize was a sniffing motion. "Yeah, I guess it would be odd for Serafina and Cinder *not* to know Echo had left, right? Aren't wolves hyper-aware of other wolves' movements?"

I looked out at the path Echo had taken. "Did Nyko know Echo was here and not care? He didn't seem that interested in the game at all."

We moved closer to the path Inigo had marked, hugging it without crossing into it, but I found it easier now that I was retracing my own path, more or less. Yes, I was sure of it. It was like Echo had been stalking me during the game.

But that would have been ridiculous. Right?

What possible reason could he have had for stalking my every move?

"Then again," I said aloud, "I *was* on my way to the Team Red headquarters. It stands to reason, if he'd been planning a sneak attack, he'd be headed the exact same way."

Yeah. That made more sense than Faine's cousin tailing me during a game when we'd been on the same side.

Broomie shook her bristles and floated back over Echo's path. We'd been finding more brown chunks of fur here and there, but she pointed to a patch of gray fur.

I got as close as I dared without heading over

Echo's path and disturbing the scene. "Do you think that was Inigo's, left while he was dropping flags?" It *was* a bit odd we hadn't encountered any of his gray fur along the path before. Then again, Echo would have been in a much greater hurry, I imagined. Inigo would have been more careful.

Of course, that didn't mean he wouldn't have slipped up here and there.

Broomie bobbed her head at the patch of gray fur and then moved closer to the ground. The pawprints nearby here seemed… smaller. Significantly smaller than Inigo's, whose pawprints I was pretty sure I could point out going in a little circle near the latest flag. They never reached over here to this bush.

"Could Inigo have missed this?" I wondered. I took a deep breath and thought about what to do. I still couldn't think of an enchantment I could cast that would help me, though I was sure if I took the sample home, there was some kind of potion that would tell me to whom it belonged—*if* I'd had a sample from each gray wolf to compare it to. But I was unlikely to get that, since everyone was done turning into a wolf for another month. And I couldn't exactly go around with tweezers plucking out fur without them noticing regardless.

"We better leave it," I said. "But maybe… Broomie, can you take just a *little* of that fur off the bush?"

Gently, using one single bristle, Broomie

removed a small patch of it and flew over. I tucked the fur into my pouch. "It could be nothing," I told her. "Any number of gray wolves could have run this way during the game and never encountered Echo. But you never know." I stared at the pawprints. They were smaller, which made me think of a kid or woman. Petra, Wisteria, Nyko, and Milah. Milah had been this way, or somewhere along this path, after Arjun had chased her. Nyko should have been in the clearing before he'd gotten this far, and I had no idea where Petra or Wisteria had been all game.

"Let's follow those footprints," I said, pointing out the smaller ones.

The gray wolf's smaller footprints went back and forth along Echo's marked path, which itself ran parallel to my own path. But they stayed a good distance away, like whoever it was had really been stalking Echo. Who'd been stalking me. Or we'd all just been trying to surprise the guards around Team Red's flag.

"The gray one's pawprints are in the wrong direction for it to have been Milah after she'd been chased," I pointed out. "They're headed *toward* Team Red's headquarters, not away from it. Whoever it… Oh." I stopped. Here the pawprints crossed with another trail of them that *did* indicate someone had been running from Team Red. Those pawprints crossed over the first set and went even farther into the woods. Broomie led the way and we followed those. They went away from Team Red headquarters—and at a fast pace. There was less care taken on this farthest path, more foliage messed up, more patches of gray fur. And then it got difficult to tell because there seemed to be a smattering of pawprints here and there that vanished into foliage or hard ground without a trace. Maybe some pawprints that were the smallest I'd seen yet, but even as I examined them, I couldn't be sure they weren't just partial prints. But I tried not to lose track of the trail. I was pretty sure those pawprints moved more carefully to the first path I'd been following, making a loop.

"Whoever this was headed *away* from the Team Red headquarters in a hurry. Then made a loop back around and moved closer toward Echo, keeping a distance but following him the same direction he went, *toward* Team Red headquarters." I looked around, noticing where I'd fought with both Draven and Roderick. "Just like I was doing." Something wasn't quite making sense.

"But this is *past* where Echo was found. He got this far? Watching our fight with Draven and Roderick? Then he retreated?" I looked around for signs of flags, and sure enough, there was another branch of them, with larger pawprints leading away.

These pawprints crossed with even *larger* pawprints and led straight to… The place where Echo's body had been discovered.

"Those largest pawprints must have been

King's," I said to Broomie, looking around. I felt a little more comfortable standing here at the scene, considering I'd been here last night as well. "Those were definitely too big to be the pawprints that ran parallel to Echo back there, on the way toward Team Red headquarters."

So King had never been around Echo during the game, not until he'd found the body? Just like he'd said.

Though I supposed a single moment would have been all he'd needed to do the job.

Broomie and I fanned out, looking for clues and trying to ignore the small pool of blood where Echo had once been.

Pawprints were everywhere, of all sizes, because everyone had come to answer King's summons.

"Look for the small ones," I told Broomie. "The ones that matched the gray wolf who ran parallel to Echo before this." After a little bit of looking, Broomie and I had it narrowed down to a couple of sets of pawprints.

"This one's alone," I said. "They didn't arrive with other wolves. Let's follow their path."

Broomie nodded, and I did my best to stick to the side of the pawprints. Here and there, there was more gray fur, and I had Broomie take a careful sample for me again, putting it in a different pouch than I had the first one. "This one loops," I said, pointing out how the path of these pawprints went right back in the direction from which we'd just come, in a wide, sweeping arc through the woods. "What if they were at the scene where Echo was *before* King summoned everyone? They took off, then looped back when everyone else did?"

Broomie nodded slowly, as if thinking it over. I indicated we should follow the sweeping pawprints back. We got no more than a couple of feet before a *snap* of foliage made me freeze.

I turned my head in the direction of the noise.

Obscured by some of the foliage, just a short distance away, there was a sleek, thin gray wolf.

And in their mouth was a wolf's vest, complete with paintball cannon.

Chapter Fifteen

"Hold it!" I shouted, with as much authority as I could muster.

Then I realized… It wasn't the full moon. Any wolf I was speaking to now wasn't a werewolf—it was a *wolf*-wolf.

"Good boy?" I ventured, freezing, forcing myself to slow down so as not to scare the creature.

I brushed the nearest branch aside and peered at the creature.

It wasn't a creature at all.

Nyko sniffed loudly, adjusting the zipper of the hoodie he had on without a coat anywhere in sight.

"Nyko?" I blinked. I could have sworn I'd seen a *wolf* here. Had it been this kid, crawling on the ground?

His hoodie *was* gray.

Nyko shook his arms out. "What?" He spoke in

such a surly tone, it was like *I'd* disturbed him in a perfectly reasonable place to stumble upon an errant teenager who was supposed to be visiting the local school.

"What are you doing here?" I asked. Broomie slipped out of my hand and took to the air, giving her an aerial view.

"Walking," he said, slipping his hands into his jeans.

"In the middle of the woods? This far from town?" I narrowed my eyes. "Near where someone was killed last night?"

He shrugged. He was doing his best to look sullen—hunched shoulders, eyes on the ground—but as soon as Broomie got a few feet away, his head snapped back up.

She stopped, pointed down, and then there was a buzzing sound.

"Was that a phone?" I asked, pleased with myself for being familiar with the noises such things made now.

"No," said Nyko as the buzzing sound rustled some foliage yet again.

Broomie grew ramrod straight and pointed down.

"Where's your phone?" I asked Nyko. He'd been attached at the hip to it before.

"Back at the house," he said through clenched teeth.

I'd seen him sticking his nose in it when he'd entered the school this morning.

I darted around him and he ran to block my way, but now I could see what Broomie had been pointing at. Nyko's puffy, blue coat was on the ground, and it was shaking as a phone clearly buzzed again.

"Why is your coat *and phone* on the ground?" I asked him. He dived in front of me before I could bend down to pick it up. But while he was busy blocking me, he left Broomie unattended behind him. She stuck her tail end underneath and lifted the coat up off the ground.

Revealing, as far as I could see around the gangly teenager, a wolf-sized vest with paintball cannon attached.

Nyko let out a curse and straightened up, giving me access to what he'd been hiding.

"Is this… Echo's missing vest from the game last night?" I crouched near it, afraid to disturb the evidence.

Broomie handed Nyko his jacket, and he snatched it from her, sliding it on and muttering as he took his phone out of his pocket and started typing on it.

I looked at the vest. There were no paintball stains, so Echo hadn't ever been spotted by a member of the opposite team—or he hadn't been successfully targeted, anyway. That tracked with my observation that he'd seemed to be in stealth mode, running parallel to me without any signs of a confrontation along his path.

Unlike the pristine vest I'd found in Team Blue headquarters, though, this showed signs of having been worn. The Velcro was stretched, and there were wisps of brown fur amidst the fasteners. I grabbed a fallen stick nearby and poked at it.

"Wait—" said Nyko.

But as soon as the vest moved sideways—onto the button the wolves would smack with their tails during the game, I realized too late—I hit the trigger and a blue paintball went soaring out and upward.

Broomie let out a bristly shake of fear and took off as the paintball splashed against a tree trunk behind where she'd been.

"Sorry." I winced as I stood back up.

Broomie flew back down and shook her brush head, doing an imitation of someone wiping their brow as she moved the tail end of her shaft against her bristles.

I looked at Nyko, who grunted and kept typing on his phone.

"You knew the paintball cannon was still loaded," I said.

Nyko grunted again.

"What were you doing with this? You hid it from me, so you clearly didn't want anyone else to find it."

Nyko looked up and clucked his tongue. "I was

just doing someone a favor, okay?" He looked back down at his screen.

"A favor? Hiding a piece of evidence? For whom?"

Nyko didn't answer, just kept typing. I was suddenly keenly aware of how frustrated his mother had seemed over the same situation.

"ENOHP, EMOC."

His mother didn't have enchantments with which to rip the phone out of his hands, though.

"Hey!" he shouted as the phone went flying from his hands to mine.

I glanced at it. "Who are you texting? Whoever asked you to do this?"

There was a series of messages on the screen.

I miss you. I love you.

I love you more. I miss you more.

I wish you didn't have to be gone for a whole week.

My dad said I have to turn off my phone at night now because he caught me texting too much after I was supposed to be in bed. So dumb.

My mom is so dumb. Why did I have to come here? It's a really dumb little town, smaller than home, and everyone here sucks. I'm talking to a witch right now who really lives up to her na—

The message wasn't finished. I glared at Nyko, but then my thumb slipped across the screen and I hit *send*. I frowned. I'd just texted his girlfriend an insult about myself.

"Give that back! You have no right to snoop

through my things!" Nyko lunged at me, swiping at his phone.

I dodged, jumping back. "Oh? But I'm so *witchy*, so why would I help you?"

He lunged again and I dodged again, slipping the phone into one of the pouches at my belt. "I'll give it back—*if* you can answer a few questions."

Nyko crossed his arms and his lips grew thin. "I didn't do anything to Echo, okay? You saw me get out of the game. I was in the clearing after that until Uncle King howled the emergency call."

"I didn't accuse you of doing anything." I frowned as Broomie slid back into my hand, leaning forward slightly, as if ready to push against the teen if he tried to lunge at me again. "You said you were doing someone a favor. By *hiding* evidence."

Nyko sniffed and stared at the splatter of paint-ball paint on the tree trunk behind me.

"*Nyko*, I may just be some witch to you, but I'm practically a daughter to our town's law enforcement."

He sneered at me. "*Uncle Inigo* is the town's law enforcement."

"And he's going to get you out of trouble, you think?"

Nyko shirked back, wilting somewhat.

A sudden, sharp pain rang against my chest. "Did your uncle ask you to do this?"

"No!" Nyko wrinkled his nose. "Okay, but, like,

you can't tell him about this, all right? I'm supposed to be at the school."

"Yeah, I saw you there this morning. How did you get out without anyone noticing?"

He rolled his eyes. "I'm seventeen. That was baby school. I just told that wood chick I was going to check out the town library. I thought I'd slip back in before the end of the day. No one would know I'd been here." He narrowed his eyes at me.

"Well, it'd be easy enough to confirm you never showed up at the library," I told him.

"Milah's covering for—" He cut himself short.

"Your sister? She knows you're out here?"

He shook his head once, as if clearing hair out of his eyes, but his hair didn't really reach over his brow. "She went to the library with me. That stone kid and Cousin Flora, too, after I made the suggestion. Independent study while the Tree Teacher stayed behind with the littlest kids."

Roderick was at the library? With Flora? I chewed on that for a second. Vesper did send some kids to the library while she focused on other lessons, even when I'd been a student there. I just wasn't sure he and Flora were old enough, even if the library was practically next door to the school.

But I was getting off-track.

"But you actually meant to come to the woods?" I asked.

His phone buzzed in my pouch, reminding me that I still hadn't checked in with Cable today. But

I'd rather tell him about today's events when I was sure we had it all taken care of.

Assuming his mom or someone else hadn't already updated him. I frowned. It'd probably be best I stop at home sooner rather than later.

"Not at first." Nyko kicked at a pebble on the ground. "Just figured the library was a better place to use my phone than the dumb schoolhouse. The teacher kept asking me to put it away."

It buzzed again. I could only imagine why.

"You knew exactly where to find this vest," I said. "Why?"

Nyko swallowed. "She told me where it'd be and asked me to hide it, okay?"

"Who? Milah?"

Whose smaller pawprints had I seen following Echo's trail from a distance? Both Nyko and Milah were svelte as wolves, but he was right. He'd been sent to the clearing, and if everyone there could prove his alibi, then that left Milah.

Whom I knew to be in the area around the time when Echo had been killed.

But still. A kid?

"She didn't do anything," Nyko said quickly. He didn't deny she'd been the one to tell him where to find the vest.

"But she knew where to find the vest. She *hid* it."

Nyko shrugged.

"Why?"

He didn't answer.

"You didn't think to tell your parents? Your uncle? This looks bad, Nyko. For you—for her. A dead man was missing something, something your sister knew where to find."

"It wasn't her," Nyko said flatly. He sighed. "Look, Echo—I mean, he was a bit embarrassing, but he could also be cool. Milah and I both liked him. Stop trying to make Milah out to be this monster, okay? She's already—" He clamped his lips shut.

"Already what?"

"She doesn't want to get in trouble."

I sighed and stepped over toward the vest again. Why hide it in the first place?

I crouched down, less careful this time, searching the vest for any sign of Echo's wound. No clean tears, no sign of blood... But there were some indents, maybe some teeth marks on one end. It was like Echo, in wolf form, had purposefully removed the protection that might have saved him from being stabbed with a knife. Not that I was *sure* those vests could have held up to a stab, but... Oh. I stopped touching the vest when a pocketknife slipped out of it.

The handle was worn down, black paint chipped and scratched, but there was a word carved into it. A "K" maybe? There was at least another letter, but it was worn away.

Were these... initials? K and... B? Maybe that could be a "B." Half a "B." King Bane?

As I was examining it, the blade unfurled from the handle, and the silver was glaringly stained a musty, brownish-red.

Dropping the knife like a hot potato, I jumped to my feet and gestured to Nyko. "All right. Let's go see your uncle. He's nearby."

"No!" Nyko shouted. "I can't let him know."

I sighed. "Let him know *what*, Nyko?"

He dropped his head. His phone buzzed again in my pouch and I thought maybe if I gave him the opportunity to vent to his girlfriend, to have his hands flying across the screen in his endless distraction, he might distract or soothe himself and let something more slip out. I took the phone out of my pocket, glancing at the screen as I did so. There were more messages from the girlfriend.

A witch? Cool! You know they're among the wickedest paranormals out there. Be careful around her. Lexa always said she'd make a cool witch.

I froze, staring at the screen.

Another message in the thread. Nyko must not have had his phone set to bring up the screensaver after this short a time.

Lexa told me she met one before she skipped town, you know.

"Nyko, do you know anything about Lexa Bane and witches?" I asked.

But before I could even look up from the screen, the teenager had snatched the phone out of my grip, taking me totally unawares, and then he put the phone in his *mouth*.

Before I could ask why, he transformed into a sleek, gray wolf and took off farther into the woods, away from Luna Lane, in the direction of Creekdale.

Chapter Sixteen

"Broomie, let's go!" I didn't have to tell her twice. She shot under my seat and we took off into the sky so quickly, I didn't even think about using enchantments to clear the way, instead using a forearm to keep the branches from scratching my face as we shot up and over the trees.

Letting my arm down, I blinked, the cold air getting to me because my warmth enchantment must have been wearing off.

"There!" I shouted, a crack of movement from the woods below just up ahead.

Broomie nose-dived, getting as close to the trees as she dared without bringing us back beneath the treeline. With so many of the trees having shed their leaves in winter, it was a bit easier to see the dark dot scurrying through the brush.

"POTS!" I shouted, with a wave of my hand,

but the enchantment didn't reach Nyko, didn't cause him to stop.

I leaned forward on Broomie's shaft to decrease wind resistance. It took just a few seconds, but we were basically hovering right over the scurrying wolf below.

But then my eyes flicked up and I saw it: the road leading to Creekdale, the end of the invisible barrier. "Broomie, stop!" I shouted.

She turned her brush head around for a better look and seemed to realize a moment too late. She made a hard turn, the wolf not even hesitating below us as he ran beyond the barrier I had no reason to pass through.

I'd learned my lesson. And Nyko didn't appear to be in any danger—just trying to avoid answering a few questions. Besides, if he was involved in something, that was an issue his family needed to hear about.

Broomie and I started pinwheeling in the air, tumbling head over feet and head over tail as we headed downward. At least she'd managed to angle us away from the tree, toward a patch of snowy ground along the road.

I closed my eyes and focused through my chattering teeth, drawing up the stone that lived in my blood.

At first, I realized the foolishness of my actions as I felt myself falling faster, harder, as my toes and fingers turned to stone, the gray rapidly spreading across my skin. But just before we were about to crash, I felt my wings coming in from behind, pushing through my dress as if the material itself were nothing more than part of my stone skin, malleable and stretchable.

I righted myself, started flapping my bat-like wings, and reached a hand out, catching Broomie by the middle of her shaft and landing with a *boom* of my stone boots against the snow. It didn't hurt at all, though.

After the sound of my landing died out, Broomie wilted a bit, her bristles letting out a sort of sighing friction.

"See?" I told her. "Me being able to fly isn't a bad thing."

She shot out straight and out of my hand, shaking her bristles back and forth with vigor, louder than the sound of distant traffic.

"I'm not saying it was your fault," I told her, my stone tongue making sparks of sorts against my stone teeth as I spoke. "Of course it wasn't! I was so focused on going after Nyko, I didn't notice where we were until it was too late. I'm just saying we could *work* together, like we usually do."

Broomie turned around and wrapped her tail end in front of her, like she was crossing her arms. Would she have rather we'd crashed?

Letting out a deep breath, I looked around and spotted something that might distract her. "Here. Look. Some more wolf fur. This time, I know it's

Nyko's." I collected it gently and put it in a different pouch than the others. My pouch, unlike my dress, hat, and boots, was not stone. "Let's use a potion to analyze this. See if it's all from the same wolf. I didn't verify his alibi yet. Maybe Nyko wanted to get out of the game ASAP so he could sneak around and spy on Echo."

It was just then I realized I was picking up on the sound of a vehicle. Roan's pickup truck approached on the road we'd landed near, the window rolling down and Inigo Vadas sticking his head out as the vehicle came to a stop.

"Dahlia Poplar?" he shouted. "Is that you?"

I looked down at myself—still stone, even the fabric of my clothes and the frozen waves of my hair.

Filling my stone lungs with air they probably didn't need, I let out a deep breath, and with it, felt the warmth and blood circulating back into my body, the wings shrinking back into my back, the gray replaced with the peachy cream tone of my skin.

Broomie let out a little dejected whistling sound and flew back into my hand.

Leaving the car running, Inigo got out of the car and fixed both his hands on his belt. "No one told me you could do that."

"No one told me you were going to be the deputy sheriff until yesterday."

He frowned. "Jeremiah said you were helping with my investigation? Apparently?"

So much for the farmer keeping my secrets.

"Mayor Abdel asked me to."

Inigo ran a hand over his face. "And you didn't think to come see me and tell me that before you started snooping around?"

I ground my boot into the snow. "My *snooping around* has led to some important leads."

"Jeremiah told me about the wolf sounds he heard last night, how you wanted to check things out. I looked over the place thoroughly. There were signs of a coyote or some other animal snooping around his chickens. Too small to be one of our wolves—unless it was Falcon or Fauna, maybe. But my brother had his eyes on them all night, and I trust my brother with my life." He locked eyes with me, as if to see if I'd doubt him. I most certainly wouldn't on Grady's account.

"I see," I said. "That's not all, though." I gestured behind me. "I ran into Nyko in the woods just a few minutes ago and he took off—as a wolf."

Inigo scoffed. "Impossible. We only change at the full moon."

"Well, I saw it with my own eyes."

"Then you're probably too tired to be *helping* with anything, let alone a murder investigation."

I gritted my teeth. "I know what I saw." Broomie nodded, our little tiff apparently over in the face of a common foe. "I can bring you to the path of his pawprints in the woods. I can bring you to—*the murder weapon!*" It had been almost an afterthought. "I found Nyko trying to drag away the vest and paintball cannon Echo wore, along with the pocketknife that had to have been used to kill him, still dirty with blood."

"Slow down, slow down." Inigo held out both palms and pushed them toward the ground, as if I were growing hysterical instead of trying to get him to follow *a lead, either lead* at this point before anyone else interfered. "Why don't you get in the vehicle and I'll take you back to the station?"

My eyes widened.

He *did* think I was delusional.

Or he was interfering with this investigation because it involved his family. One way or another, it involved his family.

"Lexa Bane may be working with witches," I said, trying another tactic, though I had the least amount of evidence for that one. "And since there are witches after my life, I have to wonder if it's all connected."

Inigo's face grew tense and he reached for the top of the gun he kept on his belt, as if I were about to go to war with him.

I scowled.

"You don't know anything about Lexa Bane," he said, no room for argument in his tone.

"I do! And Nyko knows something about her. I have to wonder if she's connected to this case. And that might mean she's involved with witches. Other witches."

My voice died down as Inigo's grip moved from his gun to the pair of handcuffs dangling from his belt.

"I've heard enough nonsense. I'm going to have to ask you to come with me," he said.

"You're *arresting me*?" I asked, swallowing. "For *what*?"

"I just want to get you back to the station," he said. "No need for a formal arrest if you just quietly come back."

"You *need* to go pick up the vest and the murder weapon!" I shouted at him. He pulled his handcuffs out. "And don't *threaten* me with those! I'm a witch! You can't put me in handcuffs."

He held up the handcuffs. "Handcuffs would stop you from casting any enchantments, wouldn't they?"

Not entirely. But he didn't need to know that. I put one leg behind the other, as if ready to run. "I'm *saying* you wouldn't get me in those to begin with."

Broomie nodded.

"Is that a threat?" he asked, frowning. "I didn't want it to have to come to this, Miss Poplar, but threatening a member of the law enforcement *is* an arrestable offense."

"I'm not threatening you!" I screamed. I knew quite well I appeared more and more unhinged the more I tried to defend myself.

So I had two options.

Flee or go with him.

It didn't have to come down to a fight.

Didn't *have to*, but as I squeezed Broomie's shaft, digging my nails into the wood of her body, a part of me really wished it would.

"I know witches are generally malevolent para-normals," Inigo said in a quiet, hushed tone as he neared me.

"Oh, for crying out loud!" I slipped on Broomie's back.

"Miss Poplar, I'm going to have you ask you to surrender peacefully—"

I didn't wait for him to say more. Broomie didn't need my encouragement. We took to the sky, back toward town.

Apparently, Dahlia Poplar was now the fugitive witch local law enforcement was after. And instead of being able to run for the hills until Sherriff Roan woke up and helped me clear up this mess, I was stuck within the confines of Luna Lane.

But I wasn't going to hide. I was going to prove this new deputy wrong and solve the crime before Roan woke up. Not only would I get justice for Echo —justice his own pack member clearly wasn't eager to seek out on his behalf—but I'd get the werewolf fired on his very first day.

Chapter Seventeen

What was the dumbest place for a wanted fugitive to go?

Probably their own home.

But I thought over my options, and although I was pretty sure that in the end, Mayor Abdel and everyone at town hall would side with me, the mayor was also the stickler type who would encourage me to just *wait in the sheriff's office jail cell* and let Inigo arrest me until *it could all be cleared up*.

That was valuable time neither of us had—Inigo nor I. I just hoped that he realized he had much more important things to do today than chase me down.

"Still, we should be in and out quickly," I reminded Broomie as we landed on my front porch. "NEPO!"

The door burst open.

"Lien?" I called down the hallway, scrambling to my potions table. "Lien!"

With a *thud* and another sound of a door bursting open, heavy footfalls indicated Lien running down the hallway, the shaking bristles of Broomhelen right behind her. "What is it?" Her eyes were bloodshot and heavy, but she had her hand out at the ready. "Where are they?"

A prick of guilt worked its way down my skin. "It's fine. I'm fine. No witches or anything." At least, I wasn't entirely sure about the witch connection. "No witches in Luna Lane, other than you and I," I clarified.

She lowered her hand and frowned as Broomhelen came into the room and floated over the rune circle carved into my floor. Broomie floated up to her and the two seemed to nod in silent consultation.

I took a deep breath. "I got in trouble with the law. Just a little."

Lien cocked her head. "With your... surrogate father?"

I waved a hand. "You know he's asleep right now. With the new deputy sheriff, of course."

Lien pursed her lips. "What kind of trouble?"

"I've been investigating the murder that happened last night—"

"Why?" Lien scoffed. "Why do you always *insist* on putting yourself in harm's way?"

"I'm not—" I sighed. "Look, I know I'm not

official law enforcement. But I'm good at it. And Echo meant something to me—to Faine. *Of course* I'm not going to sit idly by while his killer is still out there."

I turned to the potions table and pulled out the three clumps of fur, setting them down with a few inches' space between each and raising my hand. "SETON YKCITS, EMOC," I said, twirling my hand in the direction of the kitchen. "NEP, EMOC."

Lien had to duck as my pad of sticky notes and a pen came flying over her head and into my hands. I started writing down where I'd found each patch of fur.

Without looking at her, I asked, "Have you ever heard anything about werewolves turning into their wolf forms outside of the full moon? During the day?"

Out of the corner of my eye, I saw Lien put a hand on her hip as she tapped her socked foot on the hard floor.

"Is that a hypothetical question?"

I didn't look at her. I didn't have time to get into specifics. "I'm just wondering if you know that can happen."

"I'm not a werewolf expert," she said after a bit. "But as far as I know, they have to have the full moon to change. Aren't *you* close friends with a werewolf?"

"I'll ask her," I said, leaving it at that. That was

something I was sure Faine would have told me before now if it were true. Unless it was some highly guarded cultural secret.

"All right, we won't discuss the fact that you clearly need another occupation beside freelancing gofer, since you won't stop interfering with every investigation in town."

I let her have her comment and focused on labeling the fur clumps.

"I take it that's how you got in trouble, though?" she asked after I didn't respond.

I turned to her, the sticky note pad and pen still in my hands. "The mayor *asked* me to help. I just didn't... *coordinate* my efforts with the new deputy."

She arched a brow.

"Only because I knew he wouldn't be interested in my help!"

She sighed and looked at what I'd been up to on the table. "What's this?"

"Right." I set the pad and pen down. "I need to go on the run."

She sent a scathing look my way.

"Only until sundown! When I can talk to Sheriff Roan. And I *promise* I'll stay within the confines of the barrier."

"That doesn't leave you much room to 'run.'"

"I'll manage." I straightened my witch's hat. "*Anyway*, I'd like you to run some kind of potion test on these samples. See if they come from the same wolf—and if there's anything else of note you can tell me about any of them."

"Such as…?"

I wasn't sure, actually. "Any foreign object, anything that might not seem at home in the woods here, any blood or other living matter."

She stepped closer to the table.

"Is that doable?" I asked her.

"Sure, I can think of something." Lien was better at potions work than I was. Her mother, wicked though she may have been, was the best brewer in the royal family, and she went almost nowhere without her potions book. Lien could use the one my mom had left behind if she needed to consult one for any info.

My eyes flicked to the onyx dagger we kept inconspicuously amidst some pens and pencils in a mug on my kitchen table.

I wasn't planning on leaving Lien's barrier, so there wasn't a chance I'd come face to face with a witch.

And also… something about relying on the weapon didn't sit right with me right now. It only truly worked if a witch was weakened with love, Eithne had insisted.

No chance of that happening with these witches.

I turned to Broomie. "Let's go, girl."

"Wait a second." Lien held her hand out and Broomhelen, seemingly reading her mind, flew straight into it, blocking Broomie's and my path out of the house.

"He's probably going to look for me here," I explained, my heel bouncing.

"Unless he assumes you're too smart to come back to where anyone would think to look for you." Lien rolled her eyes. "ENOHP, EMOC." A phone soared out from a charging station on the table by the front door and landed in her hand. "You left this on last night and I charged it for you. It's been buzzing a fair amount today."

"Cable," I said, chewing my lip. But I didn't take the phone she held out for me. If I talked to him *now*, when I was *on the run* from the new law enforcement in town, I didn't think it would do much to calm his anxieties he constantly expressed about being so far from me. "Faine or his mom must have told him about what happened last night." Ingrid hadn't been there, but news traveled fast in Luna Lane, especially news of this magnitude.

"Maybe, but I know for a fact that Draven did," Lien said.

That felt like a slap to the face. "What? Why?"

"Probably because he *knows* you and knew you'd be sticking your nose into trouble today." She gave me a onceover. "Though I can't imagine he'd have guessed you'd be in *this much trouble*."

"And he thought *texting my boyfriend* would keep me out of trouble?" I'd thought we were in a better place as friends than that. But here he was again, trying to *protect* me or control me.

"I think he just knew you would go out of your way to keep your boyfriend out of the loop. And this was important enough to let him know. Cable's friends with Faine, too."

I squeezed Broomie's shaft tightly in my hand, the coarse wood rubbing against my palm. "I would have let him know. Once we'd solved everything."

"Just take it." She shoved the phone at me again. "Talk to him."

I hesitated. I almost grabbed it. But there was a sound of a vehicle nearby and my heart was pounding so hard, I wasn't sure which was louder. "Please text him to tell him everything's okay and that I'll get in touch later."

She frowned. "*You* should—"

"Normie police can track phones!" I said, a sudden valid excuse coming to mind. "And I'm on the run."

Lien looked at the phone. "They can? Without paranormal help?"

I'd seen it on TV shows sometimes. I doubted those in Luna Lane had such capabilities—nor would they need them in such a small area—but it wasn't a *complete lie*.

"Tell him you don't know where I am!" I said, brushing past her and to the front door. Before she could reply, I took to the skies, though fortunately, the vehicle I spotted down the block wasn't Roan's truck.

Maybe Inigo really did think I was too smart to head back to my house.

"Nyko mentioned the library," I told Broomie as we headed downtown, a pain at the back of my throat. I clearly had issues keeping my boyfriend in the loop, but it was for his own good.

He was living his own life, the one he'd carved out for himself long before he'd met me.

And I could handle this on my own. I had Lien here to help with any roaming witches. This was a Luna Lane-level issue.

We came down in front of the library and headed up the few steps to the large front doors. It was a small building. A single floor, and longer than it was wider. It overlooked the park from the front, though there weren't many windows.

Inside, the librarian, a normie woman named Jane with whom I wasn't particularly close—despite the fact that this was where I'd come to access the internet until very recently when I'd accepted a smartphone and data plan into my life—looked up from her computer and nodded at me and Broomie.

As long as we were quiet, she wouldn't pay me much mind.

I didn't notice anyone at the tables up front, so I

started making my way down the stacks toward the back of the library, where I knew quiet discussion was generally more permitted.

Right before I brought myself out into the open, though, I hesitated behind a shelf full of books on ancient Rome.

I could clearly hear a hushed conversation, the voices high-pitched enough to indicate the speakers were children.

Children I recognized by voice alone.

"Why do you think she wanted it?" That was Flora.

"I don't know. I'm sorry." Roderick, his voice gravelly and youthful at the same time.

I peered over the line of books at eye level, but I couldn't get a very good look. Broomie stuck her brush head between two books, and shoved one about Romulus and Remus to the side as quietly as she dared.

"Did he notice it was still gone this morning?" Roderick asked Flora. They both had open books and notebooks in front of them on a table, but the pages in the notebooks were blank, their pencils lying atop them unused. Both had furrowed brows and sunken shoulders, and I remembered vividly their quiet consultation this morning when Roderick had—almost against character—insisted on heading to school today.

"No, I don't think so," Flora answered. "But you

don't think… I overhead Grandpa say it was a *knife wound*."

Roderick swallowed, his stony throat bobbing. "It isn't your fault."

"But if they find the pocketknife, they'll know it was me who took it."

Pocketknife?

"No, they won't!" said Roderick, nodding at her. "You didn't do anything wrong."

"That knife was special to Dad. Papa gave it to him when he got married. I just… wanted to play with it. But Mom always says I'm too young."

The pocketknife with blood I'd found tucked away in Echo's vest that Nyko had been concealing. It had been engraved with the letters K and something. That detail had gotten lost in all the activity since, but I'd thought it could have been a K and a B—standing for King Bane.

Or KV? Kodiak Vadas? Flora's Papa? But she'd gotten the knife from Grady?

One of the books Broomie had pushed aside knocked completely to the side, landing on the shelf with a *clomp*.

Both Flora and Roderick turned our way.

"Princess?" Roderick, tilting his head to the side.

I wasn't entirely sure why I'd been observing them quietly, but based on Flora's guilty expression during the exchange, I wasn't sure I'd have ever heard about the pocketknife if I'd outright asked about it.

I wouldn't have *known* to ask them about it.

I straightened up and walked around the shelf, Broomie sinking her brush head down into her shaft a bit sheepishly.

"What's this I hear about a pocketknife?" I asked.

Flora stiffened in her chair.

Roderick patted her shoulder. "She didn't do anything wrong."

Flora sighed. "No, I did. I took my dad's pocketknife without asking. I like playing with it—the screwdriver and coil part and all the little extra bits. Not the knife, really."

Roderick frowned. "She wanted to show her cousin."

"Nyko?" I asked. I looked around for Milah. I still hadn't found her, though I wasn't sure she'd stayed in the library waiting for her brother.

"Milah," Flora said. "She seemed to think it was cool, too, though she seemed… distracted."

"Distracted?"

Flora chewed her lip. "Ever since she got here. She's a lot quieter than she used to be."

Roderick nodded. "She didn't say much."

"She saw me playing with it while our family was busy arriving the other night. I'd wanted to show her anyway. I don't think her mom got one from Papa when she got married. He only had the one."

"Why did she want to see your pocketknife?" I

wondered. It didn't seem that interesting an item to me, but maybe it was to a kid who'd been forbidden to play with it.

Then again, Milah was fourteen. Surely, she could have gotten herself her own pocketknife and her mother wouldn't have minded.

"She said it was cool. Asked about the engraving on it and I said it'd gotten worn down over the years when I'd stroked it." Flora winced. "I've been sneaking that knife away for years now, just to stroke the smooth handle, mostly." Now that she talked about it, I remembered Faine had told me as much before. But it'd been a while, I thought. It hadn't even dawned on me that *that* was what she'd probably been looking for to pry apart the stuck-together LEGOs the other day. "She said she needed it and asked if she could keep it for a couple of days while visiting. I... I said *yes*. I thought it was our little secret."

"So she had it last night?" I frowned. Milah was the smallest gray wolf. Her pawprints would have matched the trail that seemed to have been shadowing Echo.

And Nyko had known right where to find the pocketknife and the vest. He'd insisted he hadn't left them there, that he'd been hiding them for a "she."

For Milah?

Milah had killed Echo?

My mouth fell open and Broomie seemed to

come to the same conclusion I did. Her bristles spread wide in evident surprise.

"Where's Milah now?" I asked, my voice a hush. "Nyko said she was here waiting for him." But before I could get an answer, I saw the shadow of movement behind a shelf. The very shelf I'd hidden behind just moments prior.

A dark eye gazed out across the stack of books, and when the figure shifted, the part of the stack that Broomie had knocked over revealed Milah's face.

"Milah?" I asked.

Her eyes widened and she took off, her footfalls loud and rapid across the library floor.

Chapter Eighteen

"Milah, I just want to talk!" I whisper-shouted. My attempts at being quieter didn't help much, though, because I still caused the librarian to shoot to her feet, a finger across her lips and a glare in her eyes, as I made my way out of the stacks after the running werewolf.

Fortunately for me, I could just make out Milah bolting outside, saving me from having to argue with the librarian about what I was up to being of the utmost importance, rules or not. And making such a scene that she might consider calling in law enforcement. Which I was on the run from right now.

I found once I got outside, though, that Broomie and I weren't alone. The door to the library opened up again and Roderick and Flora came outside.

"Get back to school," I said over my shoulder. "You won't be in trouble about the knife. I've got this."

"Milah's my cousin," Flora whined.

I focused on Roderick. "Faine would rather her kids stay safe."

He hung his head, and for a moment, his gray skin turned light brown, and he looked rather sheepish. "I would have told you eventually," he insisted. "We just thought maybe we could find out what Milah had done with the knife first. If she gave it back, then we were worried for nothing."

"We followed Milah and Nyko to the library," Flora added.

"But they both left pretty quickly after we got there. At least, we couldn't find them."

"I know where Nyko went," I told them, which was a half-truth. "Now I need to find your other cousin."

"There!" Flora pointed to one of the places where we'd made a snow fort in the park just a few short weeks ago. The fort was still there, though a few days of sun since then had warped it a bit, and the once-pure-white had been dinged by dirt and little bits of leaves and trash here and there.

Footprints in the snow led right to it.

"I'll handle this," I told Roderick firmly. "But just be careful. Nyko turned into a wolf during the day. I don't know what to expect."

"What?" Flora scrunched up her eyebrows. "That's not possible."

Roderick pursed his lips. "If my mother says it's possible, it's possible."

"My guess is witches," I said.

That was all Roderick needed to turn all-business. Flora's response was lost on her lips as he took hold of Flora's arm and dragged her away. Broomie and I took off, toward the fort.

Milah hadn't gone far. It was a wonder she'd run at all, if this was the extent of her hiding place.

"Milah?" I asked softly, bending down to peer inside.

She was still human, at least, not a wolf like her brother. She clutched her legs to her chest and rested her chin on her knees, staring in front of her —at nothing more than the snow fort wall —unblinkingly.

I got on my knees and crawled inside, and Broomie took up guard position at the opening, floating diagonally across it to cover the most space.

"Milah, what's wrong? Why were you spying on your cousin and Roderick and me talking?"

She sighed but didn't say anything. Her lips trembled and I realized she was shivering.

"MRAW." I waved a gentle hand over her, using the excuse to sit real close, and then reupped the enchantment on myself. The last bits of snow under my skirt fizzled a bit, blending in with the sodden, frostbitten grass.

"I saw Nyko," I said after a moment, when it was clear she wasn't going to speak. "In the woods."

She stiffened.

"He was trying to hide something," I told her.

"Echo's paintball vest and cannon—and a pocketknife. He didn't explicitly say, but I'm pretty sure he was telling me you were the one who asked him to do it."

Milah took a sharp breath.

"And now I realize that knife was Grady's, given to him by his father, and Flora snuck it out to play with it and gave it to you."

Milah started sobbing, burying her face across her knees. "I didn't—I mean, I was supposed to, was supposed to do… But not *that*. I didn't!"

I reached a hand out and tentatively patted her back as she took heaving, gulping breaths. "It's okay," I said, an empty platitude, but the first thing that came to mind. "Just let it out."

Could Milah have really killed Echo? This *child*? Why? She seemed cut up about it, but I imagined she would have been, accident or intentional.

She wiped her nose on her jacket sleeve and let out a deep breath.

"Do you want me to find your mom?" I asked.

"*No!*" she shouted. "She-She would never…" She gasped and cried again.

"What about your grandparents?" I said. "Your uncles?" Though I couldn't exactly go out looking for Inigo right now.

"No," she whispered, softer. She wiped her eyes with the heel of her hand. "But just-just know that Nyko was only helping me. He had nothing to do with it. I-I broke down and told him everything this morning at the school. He-He said he'd take care of everything. That it'd all be okay. But-But it's *never* going to be okay again. Not since Echo is... Echo is..." Another sob wracked her throat.

I decided to try to get her to focus on her brother. He was the one she'd been most coherent about, most adamant about protecting. "Nyko did something... strange when I talked to him," I told her.

She sat up a bit straighter, looking at me with red, puffy eyes for the first time since I'd joined her in the snow fort.

"You don't know anything about a werewolf becoming a wolf outside of the full moon, do you? Did you know your brother could do that?"

Milah pursed her lips, a sudden look of determination taking over her eyes. "I've never *seen* him do that."

The change in her demeanor didn't go unnoticed. She'd carefully chosen her words there.

"But you knew that wolves could do that? Sometimes? Somehow? Maybe only some of them?"

She deflated a bit, losing the stiffness in her spine. She'd probably thought she'd come up with a way to avoid lying outright that would go unnoticed.

But despite what her uncle thought, I had some experience with this kind of thing. And she had all the hallmarks of a kid way in over her head. I just had to get her to explain exactly what was going on.

When her reply wasn't forthcoming, I whispered, "Can *you* do that?"

She wiped her face with the heel of her hand—a little too hard, as if angry. "She was going to teach me. She must have taught Nyko today, and he took to it. He was always a faster learner than me."

I had a hard time imagining the chained-to-his-phone grumpy teenager being a faster, sharper learner at anything, but my exposure to him had been limited and very biased, considering he didn't even want to be here. He was little different than the typical kid his age dragged on some family vacation against his will.

"Milah, Nyko could be in trouble." I watched her carefully and her breath hitched at that. "He ran off beyond where I could chase—*help* him when I saw him. And he *didn't* manage to hide the vest and the knife. I couldn't get your Uncle Inigo to go after him, either. He didn't believe me about him turning into a wolf during the day."

She swallowed.

"But *you* do. You know it's possible. You said 'she' told you."

I had a name on the tip of my tongue—this nagging theory, a gut instinct, that I had no solid proof of, but that wouldn't let go—but I wanted Milah to speak it first.

"Shouldn't *you* know, too?" Milah whispered. "You're a witch, aren't you?"

My heart about dropped down to the ground.

Could witches do that? Lien hadn't seemed to think so.

Eithne is always warning you against trusting another witch, even if she'll admit Lien is better than most.

No. I *did* trust Lien. It was plausible she didn't know something that a stronger witch might have.

A stronger witch like my grandmother, Isadora Poplar. Or her sisters, Sally and Mabel—Mabel, Lien's mother. But the two were hardly close enough I'd credit my great-aunt with teaching her daughter all there was to know about witchcraft.

I'd asked Nyko about Lexa's connection to witches, too, which his girlfriend had unintentionally clued me in on via her text to him.

"Is Lexa working with some witches?" I asked Milah.

Her eyes widened as she stared me down. I wondered if she hadn't expected me to bring up Lexa.

But I'd been right. I'd been dismissed by Inigo, but I'd been right.

Unless… he knew perfectly well she was involved and he was covering for her.

"Does Inigo know she's here?" I asked Milah.

"I don't… I don't know," said Milah quietly. "You have to understand… Lexa was nice to me."

I frowned. Had Lexa manipulated this girl?

"Before she left the village, she was like a big sister to me." Milah sighed. "My dad travels a lot— and when he's home, he and Mom fight." She shrugged. "They say they aren't getting divorced, but it's not like I believe them. It's not like *them together* is so great, either."

I nodded, though I could only imagine. My parents hadn't been together my whole life, but for very different reasons.

"She was fun. She liked kids, and she took a special interest in me—or so I thought." Milah frowned. "Nyko was so close to her boyfriend, and when he was hanging with my brother, playing basketball and video games and stuff, she'd take me out for an afternoon. Cook me a late lunch. Watch movies. Tell me about her interests."

"Like witches?" I guessed.

Milah put her chin back on her knees.

If she didn't want to talk about *that* yet…

"But I've heard people say Lexa was dating your Uncle Inigo at the same time. You called Echo her 'boyfriend.'"

"We thought he was. *He* thought he was. Nyko and I knew to keep it secret. Lexa claimed her dad wouldn't approve, due to his friendship with our family and our family's rivalry with Echo's. It felt like this big secret they trusted Nyko and *me* with. Me, this little kid."

She was still fairly young in my opinion, but she would have been about seven or eight years old. That *was* a heavy burden for a kid. What had that Lexa been thinking? Or Echo, for that matter?

"Then she left the village," I said, prompting her to speak a bit more.

"She left, but not before she told me she was having a baby. By then, I knew everyone was angry at her and Echo, claimed she was 'two-timing' my uncle, which I didn't understand at the time. But she told me a secret she told no one else—not even Echo. Though maybe her dad has learned since."

King's words flashed through my mind. *"She's not his."* The baby?

"Echo wasn't the father," I said. "So Inigo…?"

Milah shook her head. "Not him, either." She bit her lip, looking at him sideways. "She found someone else to be her baby's father. Someone she… She didn't mind doing what she had to do to."

My jaw dropped. What in the *world* was this woman teaching this kid?

"Milah, did Lexa talk to you about witches?" I pointed to my hat, and even Broomie stopped watching for any approaching interlopers to swivel her brush head around. "I'm a witch. You can tell me."

Milah looked about to cry again, but she swallowed and no tears fell from her face. "Lexa wanted to be a witch! She told me I could run away with her one day to become a witch, too. At the time, I thought it sounded *fun*! But I didn't know… I didn't know…"

Witches *put an end to* their daughters' normie

fathers. My mom excepting, but she would have never been allowed to have a baby with a gargoyle to begin with, if she'd been following witch custom.

But then, what if Echo *had been* the father after all and my grandmother had found out? Could Lexa have been back to finish him off, in witch-mother, black-widow-spider style?

"Can a werewolf become a witch?" I asked, almost losing track of that main thread. "I thought witches were born."

"We thought so, too, at first," Milah said. "But Lexa met up with some. They promised her power if she converted. If her baby turned out to be a girl —because witches wouldn't accept her if she had a son."

"That's where she went," I said, whispering. "When she left the village. To witches."

Milah nodded. "In Europe. I didn't hear from her for a long time. I don't know if King did, either. But then, right before we got here…"

"She contacted you?" I asked. "But it'd been so long. You're older."

Milah wiped her face. "Yes, but I still looked up to her. I still wanted an escape. Maybe it was harder for me to believe everything she said than it used to be, but I… I…"

"She wanted you to help her kill Echo?" I whispered. Some sort of kill-the-father-of-your-child witch initiation?

Though why now? Why when he was *here*, in

Luna Lane… Right when three royal witches were after my life?

Milah took a deep breath, staring at me, then at Broomie.

"Not Echo," she whispered. "He was never supposed to…" She didn't finish her sentence.

"Milah, how does a werewolf become a witch? How can they be accepted into the witch community, gain a witch's powers?"

"By killing a witch," Milah whispered. "And you —you were a wicked, wicked one, Lexa assured me."

Broomie shook her bristles wildly as my chest tightened.

I didn't know yet how things had gone so wrong. But Milah had been sent to kill… me?

Chapter Nineteen

*B*roomie left the doorway leading out of the fort to fly in front of me, between me and the child who'd just told me she'd been after *my* life last night.

"Broomie," I said, putting a gentle hand on her shaft and trying to peer past bristles to look Milah in the eye. The girl was still hugging her knees to her chest, looking down. "It's all right. Milah's not going to hurt me. Are you, Milah?"

Milah choked on a sob. "No. I didn't think—I didn't think I could do it. But she said if I didn't do it, she had a backup plan, so I tried to stall… to stall her. By saying I'd do it. A knife seemed as good a weapon as any. It'd show her I was still planning to do the deed. I couldn't imagine m-mauling you as a wolf or anything. I never intended for it to be used."

Lexa's backup plan had been to do the job herself, no doubt.

Despite the fact that Inigo had claimed not to find any evidence of activity at Jeremiah's farm, I still had to wonder…

If every werewolf had been accounted for after Echo's murder, and yet Jeremiah had sworn he'd heard one on his farm shortly after King's howling cry summoning them all to Echo, then had it been a wild animal he'd heard?

I guessed no, it hadn't been.

"Lexa is here, isn't she? In Luna Lane." My words caused Milah's breath to hitch, and I pressed on, sure I was onto something. "She met with you at the Creekdale gas station right before you got into town—and your grandpa almost hit her on the road. She snuck in to Luna Lane and has been hiding in Jeremiah's barn, in that farm near the clearing where we set up Team Blue's headquarters."

Milah sighed. "Ye-Yes. I don't know where she's staying, but she's here. In town."

I opened my mouth to ask a question, but I hesitated, figuring out what I assumed would be the answer myself. "I would have thought every werewolf in town would have scented her last night—but maybe the witches did something to help her camouflage her scent?"

If they *didn't*, then I had to think King and Inigo, of all people, would have been *quite aware* Lexa was nearby.

"They did." Milah gulped. "I couldn't smell her

at all when I was in werewolf form. I noticed that right away. Back at the gas station, like you said. Because… Because yes, she could turn into a werewolf even outside of the full moon. So could—" She stopped herself, biting her lip.

"Your brother?" I offered. "He's seen Lexa and she's taken him to see the witches outside of town so he could avail himself of the enchantment? Have *you*—"

"No." She shook her head. "Lexa offered—she wanted me to meet her today. I told Nyko everything and he volunteered to go instead." Her lip trembled. "I didn't want him to get in trouble, too, but he insisted when I told him. I-I worried he might tell Mom, but he's good like that. He didn't want me to get in trouble. Especially since it was me who t-took Flora's knife."

Broomie—finally releasing some of the tension that had kept her body ramrod straight—floated back toward the exit, but she didn't go back to guarding it. She floated halfway between me and the opening, as if ready to fly between the girl and me if it came to blows. She wasn't totally convinced of Milah's innocence yet.

But I had a theory.

"Echo knew something was off about you, didn't he? Even if he couldn't smell Lexa nearby?"

Even though Milah's tears had abated somewhat, she still needed to wipe her nose on her sleeve. "He did."

I had to bite back a quick "clean" enchantment, especially since I didn't know her that well. And we were getting somewhere.

"I-I did my best to ignore him. To get him to leave me alone." She took a deep breath. "But as the wargame started, I could tell Echo was still concerned about me. Lexa expected me to attack you during the game while everyone was distracted and—and I wasn't doing a good job of keeping my nerves in check."

"No one else seemed to notice anything off about you."

Milah smiled wanly. "Maybe not. I'm-I'm usually pretty quiet. My anxiety may have been out of control inside my mind, but I tried to act normally. Inigo was assigned to be my partner, and he stuck pretty close. I had a hard time getting away from him."

"Until you split during Arjun's attack." I tapped my finger to my lip. "I found evidence that Echo had been sort of sneakily following me during the game. Or so I thought. Was he trying to follow *you*? Did he just come across me first?"

"He was looking for me," she confirmed. "But when I spotted him after running away from Mr. Mahajan, well, I thought…"

"Thought what?"

She looked me in the eye and nodded. "He did seem to be following you."

The second smaller set of pawprints. So they were Milah's? Had she observed Echo for a bit?

But no. Echo had seemed to leave me behind and go after another small wolf—that was when I assumed he must have run after Milah. Once he'd finally encountered her.

"I panicked. Showed him I wasn't going to hurt anybody by throwing down the knife. I could smell the suspicion rolling off of him. The worry about me. I was relieved someone I trusted had caught me, really. I wanted to expose my belly to him, throw myself at his mercy."

"Did *you* ever follow Echo?" I asked. "Like you were stalking him?"

Milah shook her head. "I didn't even know he'd left the headquarters until he caught up with me and Lexa. I—I couldn't do it. Couldn't hide behind him when Lexa was right there. I was still scared of her."

Lexa had been there last night.

It all made sense now, and I had to wonder if King had known about his daughter's involvement, too—scent or no scent. Was Inigo covering for her as well? Maybe he'd run into her at Jeremiah's farm and outright *lied* to me. He *had* gotten awfully testy about me "interfering" with the investigation after coming from there.

"Milah, I'll do everything I can to help you and Nyko, but you need to tell me *exactly* what happened."

Milah's back straightened. "Nyko didn't do anything—"

"I caught him hiding evidence red-handed," I pointed out.

She whispered, "He was doing that for me. He didn't know anything until this morning."

She'd told me that already, but Nyko seemed to be her weak spot when it came to prying the details from her.

"Why was Echo's vest and paintball cannon removed before King, Draven, Broomie, and I came across him?" I asked, clutching Broomie's shaft for moral support. The answers were so close. I just needed to coax this poor kid into confessing everything, then I could go to Mayor Abdel with information about Lexa being the killer and maybe Inigo covering for her. "I don't know if that vest could have stopped a knife, but it was pretty sturdy, so maybe. And he could have used his paintballs to at least deter an assailant." Even if it was Lexa. Even if he still cared for her. Because paintballs wouldn't have *killed* her, even if she hadn't been a part of the game and hadn't been wearing any equipment.

"Lexa took it off. She can transform into a human during the full moon, even, thanks to the witches' power."

I tried to picture it. Wolf Echo coming across Milah—shocked to find her with Lexa. He would have recognized her as a wolf, scent or no scent. But if she were a *human* during the full moon, he would have been even more surprised that he'd encountered her at all.

Because most paranormals didn't think that was possible for a werewolf.

"So she took off his vest to expose his vulnerable hide," I said. "He actually was the father of her child, and the witches suggested she kill him, just like they do with their daughters' fathers."

"No. She didn't want him dead." She sighed. "And-And at least, if she wasn't lying, she-she told me she already killed Chelsea's father. Long ago."

So she wasn't above murder. Though I should have known that, if she wanted Milah to kill me.

"Chelsea? Is that her daughter's name?"

Milah clamped up. I'd need to switch tracks or I'd lose her.

"Why else would she want to remove Echo's vest if not to hurt him?" I asked. "There's no point—"

"She hugged him." Milah shrugged, tears welling back in her eyes. "She just said she was sorry and she hugged him. She took off his vest and buried her face in his fur."

She apologized before she plunged the knife into his side?

This cold werewolf would have made the Witch Queen proud.

"So the vest was incidental. Lexa used it to hide the knife?" It felt like they could have just left it behind otherwise. We'd already known his vest had been missing. What did it matter if it was nearby?

Other than we'd verify he hadn't had it on when he'd been stabbed, but that was hardly an important clue. The knife wound itself had been clean, indicating he hadn't struggled.

Because he'd been surprised, he'd allowed his onetime love to embrace him. Having no idea how dangerous she could be.

"No, I did. I-I panicked because she-she used the knife I'd taken from Flora. I didn't even see her pick it up off the ground, but she must have. I don't think she wanted to *eat* another wolf, so she-she looked for some other way to do it. I snatched the knife out of her mouth and put it in the vest, then when I heard someone approaching, I wrapped it up and carried the vest away in my teeth."

My heart sank. She was rambling now, but there was something she'd said that didn't quite match up.

"I already told her I didn't want to do it! That I didn't care if I never became a witch—and L-Lexa said that was fine, she didn't *need* me if I didn't want to join her. She had a backup plan… A backup plan, but she didn't think. She couldn't have meant for that to happen."

Broomie swirled her head toward the snow fort's opening.

"Milah, you said you took the knife from Lexa's *mouth*. But she was in human form when she embraced Echo, right?" It seemed a convoluted way to stab him, with a knife gripped between human teeth. It'd make much more sense to use a hand to stab him in the side like that while he was distracted by the hug.

"Lexa was—"

Something crashed through the side of the snow fort, a blur of dark gray amidst the white. The whole fort began to crumble. The snow showered down around us, temporarily masking my sight with a wall of snow that got into my open mouth even as I shut my eyes and raised a hand above my head.

"Broomie? Milah?" I said between spitting out clumps of snow.

I blinked, my eyelashes still heavy with bits of snow fort.

Broomie burst out of the snow beside me, shaking her bristles out, though some snow still remained caught on the twig-like strands.

"Milah?" I asked, patting Broomie's head.

There was a growl from the largest clump of snow in front of me.

"Milah?" I waved my hand over it. Had she turned into a wolf, despite claiming she'd never been given the power to do so outside of the full moon?

"EVOM, WONS." The snow pile responded to my enchantment and the movement of my hand, lifting up into the air and tossing itself a few feet to the right.

Milah was there, spitting out snow and rubbing her eyes. Entirely human.

And beside her was a lithe, brownish gray wolf

—so sleek, it might be confused for a coyote—wearing a paintball cannon vest.

The way it stared at me, its wide, brown eyes narrowed, made me realize for a split second the snow-dusted creature clearly had me in her sights.

Her tail whapped the trigger on the cannon.

And instead of a bright red or blue ball of paint, I was positive the shiny, silver projectile headed my way was going to prove lethal.

Chapter Twenty

Broomie threw herself in front of me, and for a moment, I pictured Isadora's anguish at the loss of her broomstick.

Even she—a woman so thoroughly incapable of love—had seemed capable of it at that moment, at the prospect of losing her companion broomstick.

"EIMOORB, EMOC!"

Broomie flew into my hand and I slammed down to the ground, summoning the stone that could replace my skin, my wings growing in last of all.

Stone might have been able to handle a heavy projectile better than flesh, but I knew that statues still crumbled.

I took to the sky, the small cannonball just grazing my stone boot.

A little bit of stone pebbled off from said boot. I

really hoped that meant I'd turn back into flesh and be missing the toe of my boot—not my actual toes.

"Milah!" I shouted down at the girl, who was standing now, looking down at the svelte wolf, looking up at me, her jaw agape. "Go get help!"

The wolf turned her head and snarled at the girl, but that only seemed to motivate her to run faster. She took off through the park, not even bothering to look behind.

The wolf I assumed had to be Lexa stared in Milah's direction a moment but then let her go, looking up. She revealed her teeth, emitting a low growl, then brought her tail up toward the trigger again.

"How many paintball cannonballs could the wolves load in those?" I asked. It had seemed to be more than one.

Broomie's answer was to shoot out of my hand —at least not to act as a shield this time—and slip under my seat, despite the fact that I was already flying.

The moment the wolf hit the trigger again, my broomstick careened us forward, dodging the projectile with even better accuracy than I had dodged the last.

"Thank you, girl," I said, patting her shaft. My own wings stopped flapping, and though she seemed to strain just a bit more than usual, Broomie kept us levitating.

The wolf growled.

She'd caught me by surprise. Now I had the advantage.

"EVOMER, TSEV." I waved my hands in the wolf's direction.

She whimpered and her entire body yanked in tandem with my hand. Before she could right herself, though, the vest unfastened and flew away, slamming against a tree and exploding once more in a *boom*. Bits of bark went flying and I winced.

"You're under arrest—um, citizen's arrest!" I shouted at the wolf. My stone tongue clacked heavily against my stone teeth.

The wolf gained her bearings again and growled up at me, leaping into the air—and missing Broomie and me by quite a few feet. I raised a stone eyebrow. Not to mention, unlike with a projectile, I was quite confident my stony ankles could handle a wolf bite.

"Give up!" I said, lowering slowly. "I don't know what kind of deal you think you've made with the witches, but you should be ashamed of yourself. Not just for targeting me, but for killing someone who *cared* about you, who—"

The squeal of tires drew my attention just before I landed. Roan's truck stopped at the curb and out came both Inigo *and* Lien. He'd stopped by my house, looking for me, I expected. And she'd joined him in the car? Out of the bed of the truck, Roderick took to the air, in his flying golem form. Could he have told Inigo where he'd seen me last?

Broomie's quick head shake sounded like a shrill scream and then I heard the crunch of glass.

I whipped my head around to find red dripping from the wolf's bared teeth, red splattering the ground. Had she cut herself? There was shattered glass at her feet.

My heart caught in my throat just as Broomie went stiff beneath me and we fell the last couple of feet with a thud. The tips of my fingers were already turning peach as the wolf lunged and bit into my ankle—and it wasn't like teeth against stone at all.

I screamed as the para-paranormal-covered teeth connected with flesh.

Of course the witches had given Lexa a bottle of para-paranormal to take with her.

"Broomie!" I shouted. I kicked at the wolf, but she wouldn't let go of my ankle. "POTS!" The enchantment came on instinct, and I realized too late how pointless it was in that situation.

Para-paranormal. Too often a pain in my rear. Created by two paranormals who'd sacrificed a life —to take away the powers of anyone in the vicinity.

"Stay back!" I tossed the inert Broomie as far from me as I could, toward the approaching crowd. "She has para-paranormal!"

That drew both Lien and Roderick to a halt several yards away. If she'd gotten a little closer, she could have lost her powers. Roderick would have gone inert. Neither would have been able to help me. Lien swallowed and Broomhelen's furry brush head quivered as they all looked on at me.

But Inigo didn't stop for a second, withdrawing a small pistol from his belt. "Freeze! Let her go. The both of you, don't move!"

Both of us? I wasn't exactly the one attacking someone here. Though I'd forgotten for a moment that I was a fugitive.

I shook my leg, but that just made everything hurt harder because that wolf *wasn't* letting go.

My head was down, though, and I just managed to see Roderick reach out toward Broomie. Broomhelen floated in front of him to stop him and Lien spoke—an enchantment, no doubt, as the inert Broomie floated right into her waiting hand.

At least they were all safe.

"This is your final warning!" Inigo shouted.

Then I realized he wasn't acting as if there were some wild animal. He *knew* certain werewolves could transform outside of the full moon.

"It's Lexa," I said, more to Lien and Roderick than Inigo, if the man was already helping her. "She can turn into a wolf during the day!"

Inigo swallowed and cocked the gun. "I know that's not Lexa Bane," he said softly. When the wolf wouldn't move, he shot off to the side, missing the both of us by inches, seemingly intentionally. I screamed and covered my ears. This sounded worse than the paintball ammunition by far.

The wolf let go of my leg and whimpered.

I didn't hesitate, pulling my leg back and waving my hands over it before my eyes caught the bright red of the para-paranormal. It was hopeless.

"Get on the ground!" Inigo shouted.

"I'm bleeding," I mumbled, but I complied.

The wolf did not.

She bolted, running in the opposite direction. Inigo and I locked eyes as he lowered his gun, and for a second, I thought he'd let the killer go, but he ran after it, leaving me behind.

I blinked, watching the man kick up snow, no hope of catching the racing, lithe wolf that headed across the park and to the sidewalk a block away.

Sucking a sharp breath in between my teeth, I army-crawled toward my waiting family, doing my best to wipe the wound on the snow as I made my way there to shake off any last remnants of para-paranormal.

"Come on, Mom!" shouted Roderick, transforming in a flash to his young human boy form.

"LAEH!" Lien waved her hands and repeated the enchantment. Finally, I crawled close enough and it took, my sinew and flesh threading together as I let out a sigh of relief and the pain escaped with my hitched breath.

"Thank you." I looked up. Broomie was moving again and she wrapped herself around my shoulders. I nuzzled my cheek against her bristles, not caring how scratchy they were.

I took a deep breath. A killer wolf was out there,

but she had para-paranormal coating her teeth and I wasn't sure how close we could get before we'd be powerless again.

"What happened? Why did you come with Inigo?"

"He came to the house," Lien said quickly. "I'd just finished those results you asked for. They're inconclusive without sample fur to check it against, but the three samples are from two different wolves. Nothing else of note, other than some dirt and leaves." She rummaged around in her pouches, revealing two small flasks. "I have some potions ready. If we get a sample of fur to compare it to, I can dip it and we'll see."

I laughed, gesturing down my leg. "Will that do?" The wolf who had bit me had snagged some of her fur on the lace of my boot.

"It will." Lien reached forward and took the clump off, dipping it in one of the flasks.

I looked at Roderick. "Where's Flora?"

"With her grandparents at the café," Roderick explained. "All the wolves are there—well, most of them. They're looking for Nyko."

"I told Inigo he left town," I said. "As a wolf."

"I tried to tell them you told us that, but they didn't believe us that a wolf could transform outside of the full moon. Not even with enchantments."

"It's a match," said Lien, swirling the flask. "This one matches the two gray samples labeled 'A' and 'B.'"

"That was the wolf who was stalking Echo," I said. "So it wasn't Milah—it was this wolf. Lexa. The third sample I'm not worried about." I fluffed a hand at her as I finally stood up, brushing snow off my outfit before I thought to say, "NAELC." I nodded thoughtfully. "That was Nyko's fur. I just wanted to make sure he really hadn't been involved in Echo's death, but I know the truth now. It was Lexa all along." I frowned. "Despite what Inigo said."

Roderick swallowed. "It can't be Lexa Bane. She's back there." He nodded toward the sheriff's vehicle, which I noticed Inigo was making his way toward at a jog, finally figuring out he'd have a better chance of chasing a running wolf in a vehicle, I supposed.

I stared at the front seat of the vehicle and realized there was someone else in there. Someone I hadn't noticed sitting there before.

"She's handcuffed," said Lien. "But Inigo seemed to recognize her as Lexa Bane." She lowered her voice. "She claims to know where Nyko is, but she's not talking."

The vehicle's tires squealed as Inigo made a U-turn, riding the truck up the sidewalk a little before barreling down the road.

"She confronted everyone at the café," Roderick explained. "Before admitting she killed Echo. But she says Inigo has to let her go or his nephew will pay."

Lexa had confessed.

That was what I'd expected had happened anyway.

Except that… The fur samples had matched *this* wolf.

And then I realized what was going on.

"Lexa is guilty," I said. "But not of Echo's murder. Not directly, anyway."

Chapter Twenty-One

"The other wolf is Chelsea, Lexa's daughter." I swallowed. "She'd only be, like, six years old…"

Lien blanched as she put her flasks back into her pouches. "A *child* just tried to kill you?"

"The younger a werewolf is, the more trouble they have overcoming their wild nature," I said, having helped Faine and Grady with their kids around the full moon. "But that's mostly when they're transformed."

"Only it looks like *that* kid is almost always transformed," Lien said.

Somewhere off in the distance, a werewolf howled—and it was eerily similar to King's call of distress I'd heard the night before.

Roderick tensed and Broomie nuzzled him, too.

"Lexa told Milah that to become a witch, she

had to *kill* a witch." I locked eyes with Lien, whose mouth became a grim line.

"She's not wrong, though there are a few women who've succeeded in killing a witch. Very few, though." She shook her head. "So *that* was how my mother and aunties got around my barrier this time? By sending someone who could get through the barrier to do their dirty work—and dangling the promise of witchhood over her head?"

Roderick's jaw dropped. "I should have stayed with you."

"No, you shouldn't have." I sighed. Not everything that had gone wrong lately had had to do with me, but certainly, it was trending that way more often than not.

"Lexa tried to coach Milah to do it, but when she refused, she said she had a backup anyway." I frowned. "Her own daughter."

"Didn't she want to be a witch herself?"

"I thought so. But maybe she didn't think she could get close to me—or she *was* trying to get close to me during the game. Then Echo stumbled across her, noticed she was stalking me, so he started staking *her*…"

"And he got in the way?"

I saddled up on Broomie and Lien did the same to Broomhelen.

"My guess is, if Chelsea is the one who did it and she's been in her wolf form for who-knows-how-long… Maybe she didn't know whom she was supposed to kill. Maybe she just saw her mom holding someone—because she embraced him right before he was stabbed—and Chelsea thought she was *holding someone down for the kill*. The poor kid probably doesn't care about becoming a witch. She's probably half feral most of the time. She was told to kill someone by her mom and her mom seemed to be indicating who. So she took Echo by surprise and killed him." My throat constricted, my words choking on my tongue.

"Grim." Lien took to the air, and I followed, Roderick transforming into gargoyle form again and flapping below.

That just left the question of whether or not Inigo had known everything for longer than I had and had helped cover it up, out of some affection for Lexa.

But more importantly…

"We have to go save Nyko," I said. "Lexa is covering for her daughter, no doubt, and Inigo is after the kid." But what if Inigo was *helping* them? I turned to look over my shoulder at Roderick. "Head to Hungry Like a Pup. Tell Faine everything I've told you about Chelsea, and see if they can help track the werewolf down. She's used to little wild werewolf children. She and Grady should be able to help."

Roderick shook his head. "I can't leave you, Mother. It's my job to protect you."

Broomie flew in a circle and pulled me up beside

my gargoyle-protector-kid. "It's a mother's job to protect her child. Besides, if you get help with capturing Chelsea, you *will* be protecting me." I reached out and touched his shoulder, and just my hand turned to stone, the stone-to-stone connection somehow more resonant than flesh meeting rock.

"I've got her this time, kid," Lien said. Broomhelen nodded vigorously. "Tell them we're looking for that teenage boy who's gone missing." She locked eyes with me. "I bet Dahlia knows where to look."

I nodded.

Roderick took a deep breath. "All right." With a last, lingering look over her shoulder, he flapped his stone wings and flew away.

"You know I think Nyko is with the witches outside of the barrier, don't you?" I said.

"I do. But I also doubt Isadora herself is here. She'll be in a bad place after losing her broomstick."

"I would have thought that would mean she'd be *more* eager for revenge," I said as we flew off in the direction of the forest between here and Creekdale.

"Maybe, but I don't think my mother or Aunt Sally will let her lead *anything* now that she's lost her broom. She may still be Queen, but that's in name only."

We flew side by side, the rush of wind through our broomsticks' bristles the only sound for a bit.

"If someone else killed a royal witch," I said as we approached the clearing in the woods where we'd set up Team Blue's headquarters, "just supposing," I added quickly. "Then would *they* get the boost in powers instead of me?"

"If a woman not born a witch killed a royal witch, she'd *become* a witch in her own right. But she wouldn't get the royal's powers. Royalty is born, not made. It depends which royal is killed." Lien's eyes darted to the side. "Your mother and Eithne were directly ahead of you in line to the seat of 'Queen,' so you got the boost in powers released by the vacuum in their wake. But if one of your great-aunts dies, remember that they're behind you in the line of succession now. You'd get a boost, but less of one than if Isadora died herself."

"I see." I thought about it. "But if either of my great-aunts died, *you'd* be one step closer to the 'throne,' wouldn't you? Does that mean you'd get a bigger boost in magic, too? Is that why Sally and Mabel are just as eager to help Isadora eradicate me as Isadora is herself?"

She nodded.

"Can we land here?" I asked, pointing to the collapsed Team Blue headquarters. "Re-group before we head across the barrier?"

Lien followed my lead. I waved my hands over the collapsed structure, about to cast an enchantment.

"What are you looking for?"

"STELLEP LLABTNIAP, EMOC," I said. An array of blue paintball pellets shot into the air and into my outstretched hand. I looked down at them. There were about twenty that apparently had never been loaded into anyone's rifles.

"Why do you want those?" Lien asked.

"Well, Lexa apparently meddled with one of the wolves' paintball cannons and took me by surprise. I wondered if *maybe* we could take whatever Auntie Dearest is out there with Nyko by surprise with something like this, too. It certainly won't be expected."

Lien frowned and rifled through some of the debris by hand until she pulled out a couple of pairs of goggles and some human-sized vests, too.

"I think it's time we play another wargame," she said, passing me half of the equipment. Broomhelen wagged a clump of her bristles like an eager dog might have wagged her tail. I slipped it all on and found us each a rifle, then dropped half the pellets in Lien's hand. We loaded up the little tubes at the tops of each rifle together.

Lien smirked. "You know, a witch could just deflect any of these."

"I know—and besides, they're non-lethal, too."

"Well, in case it comes down to it… I grabbed something before I left the house." Lien tapped a sheath at her utility belt. The hilt of my father's onyx pike—turned into a dagger—rested at her hip. "Do you want to take it?"

A hot breath escaped my lips. Witches were weak against that, but you had to get close enough to stab them with it in the first place. And there was that whole "love" component Eithne kept insisting was integral to defeating a witch with the onyx weapon. True, it had worked on her because she'd loved me like a mother—as well as she'd been able to, at least.

These witches didn't seem capable of love.

"You keep it," I told her. "I'm working on fighting with my own power." I flexed my arm, and for a moment, my skin become stone, then shifted back to flesh again.

Broomie didn't seem to notice as she dived into the debris and came out a moment later with one of the werewolves' vests around her shaft. It was big on her, even if child-wolf-sized, and the cannon dangled from below.

Broomhelen got excited and dived through the debris as well, coming up with a vest of her own and a couple of paintball cannonballs balanced on top of her bristles.

"I figure while the witch we face is busy deflecting paintball ammunition, she might leave herself open for another attack," I said. Broomie took a paintball cannonball from Broomhelen and managed to shove it into the cannon. It slid in with a loud *click*.

Lien readjusted her goggles one more time. "That might work. Assuming we're facing one witch instead of two."

"Or three," I added.

"I have to be right about that," Lien said. "Isadora will be in hiding. Sally and my mother will want to get stronger to challenge her for the crown. After all, once *you're* out of the way, only one woman will stand between Sally and being Witch Queen herself. And then only Sally between my mother and the title."

"Ah, our family," I said as we both took our places on our brooms. As we fastened our rifles over our shoulders by the straps, I smiled at her, though it was weak, considering the dread crawling up my spine. "Thank you for being the sanest member of the family tree, cousin. And for trusting me to help you. We've got to have each other's backs. I know I'm a bigger target than you are, but you can't do this alone."

"I know." She took to the air. "You and Draven and Roderick and Broomhilde and Broomhelen have taught me that." She leaned toward me as Broomie and I joined her in the air. "And I have to admit you're actually the sane one in the family. A sane person isn't raised by those monsters and still thinking she has a chance of taking them down."

I swallowed. "Well, what we lack in power and experience, we'll have to make up for in strategy. Game on!"

Chapter Twenty-Two

efore we passed the edge of Lien's bubble around the borders of Luna Lane, she reached into one of the pouches at her waist and tossed a flask my way. The rose-colored contents of the potion within denoted it was a power-boost potion.

She pulled one out for herself as our broomsticks hovered side by side and tossed it back in one gulp.

I popped the top and did the same to mine, swallowing past the sewage-like taste and depositing the empty flask in my own pouch for later use.

Because we *would* have a later use for things. This wasn't the end for us.

The contents went down smoothly, albeit a bit tangy and flowery, across my tongue.

And then, following Lien's lead, we crossed the border.

The feeling of going through the one-way barrier that Lien had enacted—one-way for any witches besides Lien—was like pushing through a thin film of bubble, though it wasn't anything visual. It was something far more innate.

And once I was past it, I suddenly went quiet, as if afraid the slightest noise could alert any waiting witch to my presence.

They wouldn't need noise for that, though.

I pointed to the spot where I'd last seen Nyko and Lien seemed to catch my meaning. Under her breath, she spoke an enchantment, waving her hand. After a moment, she seemed to pick up on something, leaning forward across Broomhelen's shaft and darting for some of the woods on the Creekdale side of the border.

I followed suit, Broomie moving as quietly as she dared, and when Broomhelen quickly dived between some trees, we did the same without a moment's hesitation, landing softly on the dirt floor. Lien was crouching behind a bush, Broomhelen bending and doing the same, and Broomie and I soon joined her. Slowly, quietly, Lien removed her paintball rifle from over her shoulder and pointed ahead through some of the foliage, peering down the scope. I did the same.

This wasn't actually a wargame—that wasn't the opposing team's headquarters across the way—but there was a ramshackle three-walled cabin of sorts, hastily put together without much more finesse than either wargame team headquarters. A fire crackled, a cast-iron pot in place above it, dangling from a bar with iron posts affixed on either side of the fire. The contents were boiling, steam rising into the air along with the "pop" of potion bubbles.

A few feet from the fire, a sleek, gray wolf whimpered, a smartphone cracked on the ground beside his muzzle. His forelegs and hindlegs were tied together with what looked like vines of ivy, his snout tied together the same.

My spine tingled. Nyko was just a kid.

Her back to us, there was one witch present, unless others waited in the wings to ambush us. A clever wargame strategy that would have been. My eyes darted around for signs of any hiding witch as the witch before us hummed in front of a makeshift table, a large potions book opened as she went to work with a mortar and pestle. A jagged, white broomstick sat atop the table, flapping the tip of her black-knot-dotted shaft lazily like a cat with its tail.

The witch wore yellow—yellow, pointed witch's hat and yellow, short-sleeved dress, with a golden shawl around her shoulders. I knew she'd give off the appearance of a harmless middle-aged lady who liked to stay curled up cozy by the fire knitting once she turned around, but I knew better than that by now.

Mabel looked a lot like her daughter—same straight, black hair, same narrow, dark eyes, and same tawny complexion—but I wasn't sure I'd ever seen a smile on that face that hadn't been the result of some wicked deed or conniving scheme.

Suddenly face to face with her, albeit with a number of bushes and trees between us, I was hit with a sinking feeling.

I'd taken a life in self-defense—been *manipulated* to do that by my own aunt. I felt bad about the death of Isadora's broomstick, even if it had been just as wicked as she was.

But here we were, asking for a fight that could only end one way. We'd tried just fighting them into submission. They always came back.

I swallowed. After the past two days, I'd never think of wargames as fun and games again.

I tried to speak as softly as possible. "What if we aimed for her broomstick?"

Lien stiffened beside me, as did Broomie. She probably didn't see me attacking Mabel's broomstick as any less violent and awful than aiming for the witch herself.

"Take her out of commission?" Lien confirmed. She'd said the death of her broomstick had been enough to get Isadora to retreat.

Lien swallowed. This was her mother.

Then she nodded slightly.

But in that moment, everything changed.

The sound of a distant car drew the attention of first Mabel's broomstick, then Mabel herself. Even

Nyko's head shifted from where it lay on the hard dirt.

Lien remained focused, though, gesturing with her hand for the two of us to spread out, me to take the side closer to the broomstick, her the side closer to her mom.

I'd only taken a few steps in that direction before the sound of someone *barreling* through the woods joined the sound of a vehicle, which drew closer, closer.

"She's being chased," said Mabel to her broomstick, who flew straight into her outstretched hand. I took cover as Mabel's eyes scanned the surrounding area before she turned back and grabbed an open flask full of a sparkling, green liquid. "I didn't feel anything happen, either. I'm going to assume the precocious werewolf and her offspring failed to kill our witch."

I poked the rifle barrel through the cover of trees, closing one eye as I got the broomstick in her hand within my sights. The paintball wouldn't destroy her, but it could prove the distraction we needed.

Mabel walked over to stand over Nyko, who whimpered, kicking his legs fruitlessly on the ground.

And then, just as I let a paintball pellet fly, Mabel turned, and the pellet went splat to the ground, perhaps unnoticed, because she was looking straight at the brownish gray wolf soaring toward her through the leaves with a human girl on her back.

"Let him go!" Milah screamed.

I blinked, pulling my paintball rifle back as Mabel held her broomstick above her head in the direction of the approaching children.

The wolf was Chelsea, I was sure. The little wild creature who'd just tried to kill me and yet was now baring her teeth at Mabel like Milah-the-knight's reliable steed.

Milah jumped off Chelsea's back. Instead of going to get help when I'd asked, she'd hung back and waited? Or at some point, she'd come across Chelsea the wolf before Inigo had, and she'd ridden her out here to save her brother?

Milah trembled, and her voice shook. "Release him!"

Mabel cackled, giving witches everywhere a good—or bad—name. "Why would I do that, little wolf? Have you killed the town's witch, like your mentor asked you to?"

"No." Milah bit her lip and her eyes flicked to her brother as a wolf on the ground. He whimpered and kicked his legs. "She wasn't wicked, like you told Lexa. *You* are!"

Mabel laughed and laughed, and even her broomstick got in on the laughter by shaking its jagged, pointy bristles. "You silly child. *All* witches are wicked. And if they're not, well, they aren't really good witches, are they?" She gave her a onceover. "I think you're not built sturdy enough for such things. At least with that wild child, keeping her a wolf for so long, she's malleable, and she's used to her *darker instincts*." Mabel's eyes lit up as she spoke.

"You and Lexa did bad things to Chelsea." Milah pet the wolf's back. "Bad things. But she understands now, right? Sometimes even mommies can do bad things."

The little wolf looked up at Milah, and then she nodded. With a mewling howl, she transformed into a little girl. Wild, matted brown hair. A pale complexion. Bare, dirty feet. She only came up to about Milah's shoulders.

It was a wonder that little girl had ever tried to kill me. That she could have killed Echo.

I swallowed and Broomie nudged me. Right. The broomstick. I refocused my rifle's sights.

Milah gave Chelsea a side-hug.

"I can still become a witch," the older girl said. "If I kill *you*. Which I will do if you don't free my brother!"

Mabel snorted. "You had a slightly better chance when you had a wolf to help you fight. *Slightly*. How in the world do you expect to do that now, you fool?" She sneered. "You don't have it in you."

Somewhere nearby, wherever the road was closest, a vehicle's tires screeched to a halt.

"You're-You're all alone! And I have Chelsea.

We'll-We'll do it! We will!" Milah barely seemed able to convince herself.

But Mabel didn't move. "Besides Broomhiko here, I *am* alone," she said, and I still wondered if she was lying. The broomstick was undulating wildly in her hand and I wasn't sure if I'd get a good shot. "One of my sisters—my *queen*—is disgraced, and the other has trusted me with this task of ours while she keeps an eye on her. And I *will not* return empty-handed."

"I don't care if you're a princess, you're a wicked woman!" Milah shouted.

"Wicked!" Chelsea reiterated. Her face scrunched up, like Mabel smelled bad.

"Do you know what this is, girls?" The older witch shook the flask in the air over the whimpering Nyko. "It's a *putrefaction* potion. My absolute *favorite*." She let one drop fall right by Nyko's feet. The ground began to sizzle, a leaf disintegrating into ash.

Milah gasped and Nyko rolled, trying to get away from the steam in the air. One foot stretched and grew hairless, turning into a human-foot-shape, but the vines at his legs wrapped around it, as if fighting the transformation.

Mabel looked down at him. "I told that boy he could try to transform back into a human, but those vines would still keep him *tied up*. But maybe he can't hear well. Maybe I should just—oops." She pretended to drop the flask, but then she caught it. Broomhiko snickered.

Nyko whimpered and grew still.

"Stop!" Milah said. "What-What do you want from us?"

"I want a *dead Dahlia Poplar!*" Mabel shouted. "And if you're too weak-willed to do it yourselves, you at least need to *bring her to me*. Go back. Tell her I'll only exchange wolf boy here for her head—"

With a *crack*, there was a smacking sound, followed by a shattering of glass, and then something crashed on the ground.

Mabel's and Broomhiko's heads whapped toward the makeshift potions table.

"My book!" shrieked Mabel. It had fallen to the ground, a splattering of blue paint on its open pages. The cannon on Broomhelen's shaft had steam coming out of it.

"My precious book!"

Broomhiko had finally stilled enough that I aimed and fired a paintball pellet of my own.

Blue coated the white broomstick's bristles, stickily dripping downward.

"My baby!" shrieked Mabel.

"KOOB OT DAERPS, ERIF," Lien said, jumping out into the clearing, shooting off her paintball rifle with wild abandon at the same time.

With a wave of her hand, some of the fire crackling beneath the boiling cauldron flew to the book her potions-expert mother was exceedingly fond of. It caught on fire.

Broomie and Broomhelen spread to either side of Lien and both whapped the tips of their shafts against their vest buttons, sending paintball cannonballs flying in a riotous attack, paint splattering everywhere. Milah and Chelsea shrieked and ran away.

Mabel shrieked and ran away from Nyko and the girls, falling to her knees in front of the book and shouting enchantments in vain. She put out the fire fast, but the book was black, missing in parts and stained with ash. A paintball cannonball splattered against her back and she barely seemed to notice.

She shouted more enchantments and I moved quickly to Nyko's side, shouting a few of my own. "EVLOSSID, SENIV!"

Nyko was free. He transformed quickly into a human, jumping to his feet and throwing himself in front of the girls.

"Go," I said to the three of them, locking eyes with Chelsea. She swallowed and hid behind Milah, peeking out around the older girl's legs. "I think I heard your uncle or someone stop by the road. Head that way—"

There was a high-pitched scream.

I whirled around.

Lien's paintball rifle hit the ground with a *thud* as her mother held her up by the neck, Lien's toes just barely grazing the ground. Lien's hand flailed wildly at her hip, reaching for the onyx dagger and never quite grasping it.

Beside them, Broomhiko wrestled with a vestless Broomhelen, pushing my cousin's broomstick closer and closer to the open flames.

Chapter Twenty-Three

Broomie smacked her vest button, but her cannon seemed empty. Letting out a bristly growl, she slipped out of the vest entirely and took off to help Broomhelen, just as I let the flesh of my skin turn to stone. With Chelsea no longer trying to take a chunk out of me and apparently cleansed of all para-paranormal, all I had to watch out for were Mabel's enchantments and potions. And right now, she was occupied trying to destroy some of the only likable family I had left.

Broomie trusted me to handle things—without jealousy over the fact that I could now fly without her. And I trusted her to save Broomhelen.

"OG TEL!" I shouted at Mabel as I flapped my stone wings, barreling toward her.

Though she clearly resisted, my power and focus won out, her hand loosening enough for Lien to get free, collapsing to the ground as I braced myself for a barrel roll and brought Mabel tumbling down with me.

The open flask that was in her hand fell to the ground, rolling and turning leaves and dirt into ash as it spread out along the way.

There was no para-paranormal here so that potion had probably been the most dangerous thing standing in my way.

Assuming she really was alone. I drew back my stone fist, staring down at the witch I had pinned beneath me. Anger at Echo's death boiled up inside me—anger on behalf of Draven for what these witches had done to his mother, for everything they'd put my own mother through—and I wanted to smack my stone fist against her jaw.

One less witch royal. One less threat.

But I hesitated too long. I couldn't bring myself to brutalize her—not even *her*.

"KCAB YLF!" she shouted, waving a hand up toward me. I soared into the sky, flying backward.

My current height gave me a good view of the broomsticks all tangled up. Broomie and Broomhelen were now winning, it seemed, pushing Mabel's Broomhiko toward the flames.

Lien was on the ground, grasping at her throat.

I managed to stop spinning, flapping my wings to right myself upward. "LAEH!" I waved my hands toward Lien.

Being choked seemed to have robbed her of her own enchantments.

She didn't hesitate once my magic had taken effect. First, she took out the onyx dagger and tossed at her mother. Even crouched beside the potions book on the ground, her mother easily deflected the dagger with an unspoken enchantment and a wave of her hand, but that had clearly been just a distraction. Lien waved her hands at the potions book again as her mother whispered enchantments into it in a clear attempt to fix its pages.

"NRUB!" Lien shouted.

The book caught into flames again and Mabel shrieked.

As she worked to put out the fire, Lien got to her feet and whipped around, toward the tangle of broomsticks.

"EDLIHMOORB DNA NELEHMOORB, EMOC!" she shouted, waving hands that caught our broomsticks as her eyes widened and she tilted her head toward the remaining jagged broomstick so close to the fire.

I swallowed. "WORG, ERIF!"

The flames beneath the cauldron surged up and outward in all directions, catching Broomhiko on fire.

Mabel dropped her now-smoking potions book and shrieked again, running at the burning broomstick.

I kept my hands in the direction of the flames, swallowing back my guilt, the tear escaping from my stone eye turning to stone, like it had been chiseled onto my cheek. "SEMALF, WORG!" I shouted, and the fire grew bigger, giving Mabel no chance of saving her broomstick, who was little more than ash.

But she didn't seem to stop to think about that as she moved forward and the flames met her—and she shrieked one more time, slowly, tortuously turning to ash beside her companion broomstick.

I gaped, my hands lowering and the enchantment at an end.

But I snapped back to attention when someone shouted, "Fire!"

Lien was standing tall, her eyes closed, her arms stretched out with one broomstick in each hand. Her hair flew up from beneath her witch's hat brim, and I realized, a moment before a surge of power hit my own body, that Mabel was gone, and the royal witch's power was transferring to the other heirs. Lien seemed to feel the main boost of it, since she'd just gone up a number in the line of succession.

"Everyone, get back to the road!"

It was Inigo down below, his gun unholstered and pointed at Lien—who looked a little ominous right now, I had to concede.

Still, it just made me more suspicious of Inigo that he would continually lay the blame on the Luna Lane witches' feet.

The kids were nowhere to be seen, and I had to hope they hadn't witnessed Mabel's demise.

Behind Inigo, though, Faine and Grady popped

out from the woods, followed by their parents, Cinder, and Serafina. Perhaps Petra and King had run into the kids on the way here and were with them now at the side of the road.

Faine and Grady approached Inigo from behind, Grady reaching out to lower his brother's arm. Inigo's nose scrunched up and he started shouting something as he looked over his shoulder at his brother, but I used the opportunity of his distraction to turn my attention to the roaring fire that *I* had sent out of control. I was even more powerful now.

"SEMALF ESEHT HSIUGNITXE, NIAR!" As Luna Lane's resident fire brigade, I wasn't unused to fighting fires. A gush of water fell from the sky, tackling the fire and causing it to sizzle and snap into the air.

Lien joined in, too, letting the broomsticks fly and waving her hands to repeat the enchantment. Broomhelen floated between her and Inigo while Broomie flew up to block any path Inigo's bullet might have taken if he decided I was a fugitive threat worth shooting after all.

But our enchantments worked, and the fire stopped, a deep, gashing wound in the forest here, at the center of which were the blackened bones of one of the three royal witches who wanted me dead.

Inigo finally stopped arguing and stared straight ahead. Sighing, he holstered his gun and I flapped my wings down to the ground.

Inigo reached for the handcuffs at his belt but didn't draw them out. "I'm going to need you two to come down to the station. But I suppose there's no threatening you, is there?" he asked me as Faine ran over and gave me a hug, taking my stony form into her arms.

Faine growled, despite her human form. "She didn't do anything wrong. This was clearly self-defense."

"And Mabel kind of did it to herself," I said, swallowing. "Well, I did kill her broomstick intentionally." Broomie rubbed her brush head across my cheek. I let my stone turn back to flesh, just to feel the soft scraping of her bristles.

Lien walked up beside me and took my hand on the opposite side of Faine. "She saved my life."

My eyes flicked over Inigo's shoulder to Serafina, who was talking in hushed voices to her sister and brother-in-law, every so often her gaze flicking back to Kodiak and Wisteria some feet away.

"And I know what happened with Echo," I said. "It wasn't Lexa. Not directly."

Inigo sighed. "I was afraid of that."

"You were?" I raised a brow. "You weren't covering up for Lexa and her daughter?"

Faine gasped.

Inigo's nose wrinkled. "I most certainly was not. I didn't even know Lexa was anywhere *near* here until she suspiciously showed up, claiming to be guilty." He scoffed. "Like she'd do that if she weren't covering up something worse."

"You didn't see any signs of her at Jeremiah's farm?" I asked.

"I saw signs of a coyote. Maybe two. I suppose that was Lexa and her daughter. I didn't even consider werewolves would be able to turn to wolves outside of the full moon."

"But you concede that's possible now, right?"

Inigo frowned and changed the subject. "All that aside, I'm tired of everyone walking on eggshells around the topic of her. I'm over her. I've been over her for quite some time." He glanced at what was left of Mabel. "I certainly would be over her now, considering her obsession with witches."

Grady slapped a hand on his brother's shoulder. "But you never told us. You've never dated anyone else. The whole family just assumed—"

"We live in a small village, Grady. Options are limited. I had more important things to do." He pulled out the handcuffs and dangled them out toward me. "Like policework. Ladies?"

Lien and I locked eyes and I shook my head.

"We're coming willingly. You know cuffs won't hold us anyway."

Inigo smirked. "Maybe not. But if there's one thing I've learned from one *very* harrowing day as Luna Lane's daytime deputy sheriff, it's that this town could really use some law and order. And I may not have the

power to do much on my own, but with a little help…"
He put the cuffs back on his belt and gestured into the
woods in the direction of the road. "Maybe I can get to
the bottom of the crimes in Luna Lane after all."

I grimaced and squeezed both Lien's and Faine's
hands before grabbing hold of Broomie and
walking that way.

Flying would have been faster.

But I didn't want Mr. Law and Order to think I
was trying to get away.

Besides, it was best we get back to town and the
safety of Lien's anti-witch protective barrier, once
she could recast it after I had to get back in.

Because we weren't the only two witch royals
who would have been hit with a burst of power
just now.

"I just need to get a couple things," Lien said,
passing her mother's skeleton without a further look.
She bent down and grabbed first the onyx dagger,
slipping it into her sheath at her hip, then the
potions book her mother had held so dear, charred
and singed and likely now missing quite a few pages,
but at least partially intact.

"And I'm going to need to cast some enchantments so Dahlia can get back into town, and then
we can keep other witches out."

Inigo frowned. "So they can just coach another
paranormal to come in and do their dirty work for
them again?"

Lien arched a brow. "You'd rather we take a

witch fight to Luna Lane's streets?" She gestured to the chaos all around us, to the overturned cauldron leaking something putrid and purple onto the floor.

"Point taken," Inigo said gruffly. "Witch, do your thing. I'll see you back at the station." With great, wide steps, he stepped up behind me and grabbed me by one arm, pushing me forward.

I bristled at the touch, at the force with which he shoved me onward.

Mr. Law and Order certainly had to *feel* like he had control.

Because if I hadn't been in the mood to cooperate and Broomie hadn't understood the slight shake of my head I gave her not to fight him on it, he'd be shaking that hand out like a bristly rubber band had hit him.

Chapter Twenty-Four

"Lia, Lia, Lia." Sherriff Roan Birch—Luna Lane's *real* sheriff—walked into the sheriff's office from the front door, the sun having obviously set outside. "Sounds like you've had quite a day."

"I'll say. If it weren't for the fact that our only cell is occupied, your deputy might have put me in it." I winced as I looked over at the singular holding cell in the entire town, which currently held Lexa as its occupant. Chelsea had recognized her grandfather—he'd visited them from time to time before—and she was currently with him at Draven's house, or so Faine had explained when she'd swung by to update us.

Lexa was lying still on the cot, staring up at the ceiling, without saying a word. She was beautiful but cold, her full, dark lips in a permanently sour expression. Her long, lithe body was a bit longer than the cot provided, and her wavy hair spread out wildly above her head.

"So I heard. A fugitive from the law? Hi, Lien." He nodded at my cousin, who was seated across me in front of Roan's desk. I had taken to waiting for Inigo between the various tasks on his to-do list right in the chief's desk chair.

"Hi, Sherriff Roan," she said, straightening up. "We've given our statements." Her eyes flicked to Lexa inside her cell. "We recommend Chelsea be put in her grandfather's custody, but Inigo isn't keen to let her leave. She's just a kid."

"Abdel and I will see to all of that. He's on the phone with the werewolf village's mayor right now. Since it's not a normie matter, we're both of the agreement that we can do this without involving normie channels. King's promised to take custody of his grandchild and raise her better, with a little help from some therapy back home. They're keen to handle the prison term for their wayward citizen, too, even if her crimes were committed elsewhere."

All our eyes flicked to Lexa in her cell, but she still wasn't talking. She hadn't said a word to me since she'd laid eyes on me.

"Sounds right," I said. "Chelsea didn't know what she was doing. She's half-wild, being raised to stay in her werewolf form with a rare witch potion like that so much of the time."

"My mother was one of the few who knew such a concoction existed," Lien explained. Broomhelen, who'd been curled up on the desk between us along-side an exhausted Broomie, flew up over to the charred potions book Lien had brought with her. She flipped to a page, which was half-destroyed. But it was intact enough to reveal the "Werewolf's Delight" potion, which Lien had ascertained was able to give a werewolf control over when to shift into wolf form. Which Mabel had to have been providing to Lexa for years, ever since she'd sought witches out in Europe.

Now, without anyone able to make the brew, Chelsea, Lexa, and Nyko would soon lose that ability. How soon, we couldn't be sure, but Lexa hadn't transformed back into her wolf form yet.

"I bet Inigo isn't happy about passing on jurisdiction like that," I said.

Roan shrugged. "That didn't bother him too much—though letting you off with a warning for running from him seemed to get under his collar a bit."

"I bet." I rolled my eyes.

"I mean it, Lia. You have to get used to the new deputy in town. It's a consequence of my decision to become paranormal."

I reached across the table and took his cold hand in mine. "I don't blame you. I just wish I had free rein to investigate when crimes happen, too."

"Well, Mayor Abdel talked to Inigo about that. You have his express permission to help with all investigations, and I gave my blessing, too."

Lien smiled and nodded at me. I felt myself flush with all the eyes turned on me. "What?"

"Just admit that makes you happy," said Lien.

"I don't want to be a deputy sheriff or anything," I said.

"We're actually thinking of calling you a 'consulting detective,'" Roan explained. "No need to deputize you."

"Oh." I said. I *did* like that idea. "I'll… I'll try to stay out of Inigo's way."

"Don't forget the *consulting* part," Roan said. "If it comes down to it, I hope the two of you will work together."

I rolled my eyes and stood. "Well, let's just hope it doesn't come to that."

Roan slipped his thumbs under his belt. "Working together?"

"Maybe there won't be any more crimes in Luna Lane," I said. Lien and I locked eyes and I shirked. "Well, we can hope, anyway."

The door burst open and in came Draven, navigating around the cramped furnishings with big, bold steps that echoed loudly on the linoleum floor. "Lien! Dahlia!"

He reached Lien's side and hugged her, then kissed her, too. Lien's eyes went wide, but she didn't fight back.

"I heard what happened. Oh my goodness!" His Transylvanian accent was thick. "You put yourselves in such danger!"

He seemed to be speaking to both of us, but he only had eyes for Lien just now.

"We-We're fine," she said, her eyes lowering, clearly not used to someone lecturing her for putting herself in danger, like she'd done for months to me.

Draven, like Lien herself in such cases, was not appeased. "You shouldn't have taken such a risk! And you lost your mother!"

Lien looked to the side. "I *hated* her—"

"But still. My paramour…" He held her tightly, putting a hand on the back of her head as the top of her witch's hat smashed against his cheek. Finally, his eyes darted to me. "Glad you're okay, Dahlia."

"Thanks." I offered him a flittering smile, my chest growing tight at the sight of them together. But only because it reminded me that a part of me was across the ocean, so far away.

"I don't suppose I could be excused?" I asked Roan, taking hold of Broomie and heading around the desk.

He sighed and switched places with me, going to sit down. "You may, Lia. But try to keep your nose clean for at least another few days? You're on thin ice with my deputy."

"I'll keep that in mind." I shook my head.

Before I could leave the office entirely, though, a deep, alto voice carried out across the room.

"They won't give up, you know."

I turned to find Lexa standing, finally not lost in her own little world. She gripped the bars of the jail cell and looked straight at me. "They want you dead."

"That's not news to me." I turned on my heel, Broomie nodding vigorously beside me.

"I wonder what the Queen of Witches' newest plans might be?" Lexa asked.

I stopped. "If you want to tell me, tell me."

Lexa cleared her throat. "I might be willing to talk—if you let me go."

Roan laughed from behind me. I whirled around.

"Nice try." I locked eyes with Lien, who nodded, still in Draven's embrace. "My cousin and I have it covered."

"It's not your cousin you should be worried about," Lexa said. "Queen Isadora and Princess Sally went back home. Only Princess Mabel stayed behind."

"Well, *Princess* Dahlia hopes they never come back." I sneered at her.

Roan frowned. I hadn't exactly brandished that title around town much.

"Isadora wants a new heir," Lexa said. Apparently, she'd be willing to talk *some* without a deal.

"She told me," I pointed out. Still nothing new.

"Princess Sally doesn't know. She told me in confidence."

"She told me her sisters wouldn't want her to have more kids, too," I said. "You're really not helping me any here."

Lexa shrugged. "Get me a deal."

Whatever nefarious plans she was keeping close to the vest, I'd just have to go on without knowing. "I couldn't even if I wanted to." I shrugged. "I'm just a consulting detective, lady. And you deserve a very long stay in prison. Nothing you could offer could change that."

"Don't say I didn't warn you." She let go of the bars and backed up.

I noticed she hadn't mentioned her daughter in any of this. A witch wannabe if ever there was one. "Chelsea will be better off without you."

I walked out before I could hear if she had anything more to say.

Hungry Like a Pup was packed despite the late hour—the café would have normally closed hours ago. I'd leaned my tablet up on the table as I chowed down on one of Frieda's chicken salad sandwiches. She added a bit more pepper than Grady did, and Jonathan's tomato soup was a little thinner, too. Weird how my taste buds picked up on the slight changes, but I was suddenly filled with a sense of nostalgia to my childhood and to when Faine's parents had run the café.

After school, Faine and I, along with the Mahajan boys, would do our homework together in the café, munching on snacks or sometimes a full dinner. Some days, Mom and the Mahajans would join us, and we'd all dig in together—three happy families, not a care in the world. Well, at least that was how it'd felt. I supposed my mother had had *a lot* of cares with the way her family had treated her. She'd just been good at hiding it all from me.

Faine's kids were all gathered at a table across the café now, Roderick with them. He kept glancing at me every so often, but then something one of the other kids said would draw his attention and he'd smile—a big, broad smile on his human-flesh face. He'd been relieved to hear I'd fought against one of the wicked witches after me and *won*. Perhaps he'd feel just a touch less protective of me now.

Milah and Nyko were with their mom the next table over, in no mood for fun and games with their cousins. Petra was talking to them, every so often offering one a hug. Nyko seemed a bit out of it, no phone to distract him as he picked at his food. Wisteria slid in beside Milah with another plate full of food and gave her a quick hug, too.

At the counter, Grady and Kodiak talked, serious looks on their faces, as Faine sat with her aunts in the corner booth. Serafina's face was crestfallen, the food in front of them mostly untouched, too. They were going to arrange a burial for Echo back home. He'd never transformed back into his human form. That was what happened to wolves lost in wolf form, I'd learned, but there was a special ritual for those lost to wargames, a ritual that dated back hundreds of years, that Echo would qualify for.

At least that had landed a small smile of evident pride on his mother's face, albeit a fleeting one.

Since the culprit in his death had been a child—and not a wargame participant, to boot—the punishment had been waived. Lexa would answer for the crime, but she wasn't supposed to have been involved in the wargame, either. She would likely serve time instead of paying with her life to answer for the lost life.

King and Chelsea weren't here, though. Wisteria had gone to bring them some food a little while ago, but they hadn't come back with her. Maybe King had figured the pain was too fresh for everyone, and he was introducing Chelsea to society slowly.

They'd figure it out. King had never given up hope that his daughter would rejoin society, he'd admitted gruffly. Now he'd been devastated to learn just how far she'd fallen, but there was hope for his granddaughter yet.

"Dahlia? You okay? You seemed spaced out there."

Cable was on my tablet screen. I'd told him *everything*. He hadn't been happy. That was mostly what our calls were like ever since he'd left, it seemed. News about me having been in danger and not telling him about it until it was over. Me assuring him I could handle it. Him insisting he come back. Me forcing him to stay. The truth was, a part of me wanted him back. But his mom was staying with his uncle through the semester—and that would make it the perfect time for him to choose to come back if he wanted to. He owed his university this last semester at least. He loved his job.

And now I had one of my own, more or less. I hadn't discussed any pay, freelance or not, but I didn't really need to worry about it, anyway.

Maybe Luna Lane wouldn't even be in need of my consulting detective services again.

One could hope.

"Yeah, it's just… Just been a long day." I shoved the rest of my sandwich in my mouth. I hadn't stopped to eat since brunch.

"I can imagine." He sighed. "Not exactly the first Valentine's Day together I wanted for us."

I laughed. "Well, it wasn't much of one without you to begin with, but it was fun. Until it wasn't." Beside me, Broomie munched on a cornhusk and let out a sorrowful groan. "All in all, though, I think we had a pretty decisive victory. Something to celebrate at least."

Because I *was* a witch at heart. I should get used to celebrating my kills, apparently, intentional or not.

"What do you suppose Lexa meant, about your grandmother wanting another kid?" he asked.

I still hadn't told him about me being a long-lost

witch princess. He knew enough to know my grandmother didn't approve of my gargoyle blood and wanted me dead. I didn't want him worrying about me becoming some wicked Witch Queen someday.

"She told me that before." I shrugged as I picked up my soup spoon. "She just has to find a father for her kid—one she'll end up killing someday."

He shuddered. "Even Spindra wouldn't be so cruel."

"Our local spiderwoman never devoured anyone she'd sired a child with, no." Long before she'd moved to Luna Lane, she may have killed a few lovers along the way. I'd never pried. Paranormal nature was just too cruel sometimes.

But it wasn't that way in Luna Lane. It wasn't supposed to be that way, anyway.

"I pity the man who falls for her," he said. Then he winked at me. "Though since beauty runs in the family, I can't say I'd blame him for being tempted."

I rolled my eyes. "Did you try to compliment me in the middle of a joke about my murderous grandmother?"

"Maybe?" He winced. "I'm not exactly a comedian…"

"I get it. You try." I laughed anyway, resting my spoon on the table. "And if you can't laugh at the ridiculousness of the situation, you can only give in to despair. I appreciate you trying to keep it light." I yawned.

"I think you need to get to bed," he said.

"Yeah. Long, long day," I repeated. "We'll chat tomorrow?"

"We better," he said. "Every time you're late to contact me, I'm worried you're in danger. And every time I'm right."

"Not *every* time."

He shook his head. "I love you, Dahlia."

My toes curled in my boots. "I love you, too." I blew the screen a kiss. Then Broomie jumped up from her chair and burst between me and the screen. Cable let out a little cry of surprise.

She giggled.

"Good night, Broomie," he said.

She flew out of the way.

"Good night," I said, and then we ended the call.

Broomie was finished with her cornhusks, but I still had a bit of soup left. I hadn't gotten more than a few bites in before a voice hovered over from behind me, and I dropped the spoon with a clatter to my plate, causing even Broomie to jump in place.

"Dahlia, quick! You've got to come with me."

I turned around. No one was there, but I recognized Ginny's voice.

"Why aren't you showing yourself?"

"I wasn't sure if he'd want his family to see. It might cause him to leave even earlier."

"Who?" I asked.

"Just come outside. Broomhilde, fly your witch over to Draven's place. ASAP."

Broomie and I stared at one another but shrugged.

"Got to grab something at home," I said to Faine as I passed her booth. I'd left my tablet on the table. "Watch Roderick for me for just a bit longer?"

"Of course," she said. I didn't linger to explain.

Outside the café, I got on Broomie's back, and she lifted us both to the sky, making a beeline for Draven's home.

"Did Draven send for her?" I asked Broomie. The noise she made sort of sounded like, "I dunno."

As we approached the Victorian-style manor, I caught sight of movement in the back yard. Bundled up in a jacket, hat, mittens, a scarf, and boots, little Chelsea was running around in the snow in her human form, King sitting with his shoulders hunched on top of a stone bench covered in dried, crackling vines. Chelsea stopped to itch the back of her ear and tried to lift her boot to act as the scratcher.

"Use your hand, dear," said King. His voice was solemn but not too grim. "Easier to do that way when you're not in wolf form."

Chelsea frowned but took off one mitten and scratched the back of her ear. The tension in her body seemed to melt away.

"Did King want to see me?" I asked Broomie.

"Shh!" That was Ginny. I could see her now, situated in her spectral, white form on the roof. "Over here!"

I landed as quietly as I dared on the roof, and though King looked up at the sound, I didn't think he saw us.

"What's this about?" I asked Ginny. She pointed toward the back of the yard, at a hedge that separated Draven's yard from Faine and Grady's.

A wolf's shiny, white nose poked out from between the thick, green brush.

"Cinder?" I wondered. She was the only white wolf I knew of.

Ginny *tsked*. "No corporeal wolf would fit *inside* the hedge like that, without even shifting any of it in any way."

She was right. I peered closer. It was a *ghost*. The ghost of a wolf.

"Echo?" I whispered.

Ginny nodded. "My darling Lazarus sensed him almost right away. I came to confirm, then knew I had to come get you."

"Why me?" I asked. "His mother—"

"He and his mother got along great. He has no regrets concerning her." She nodded, as if she could just sense such a thing from the ghost. "You asked about ghosts and regrets, well… I thought you'd like to see."

"But that's… That's sad. He's going to be here

as a ghost? I mean, we can keep him company, but…"

Ginny shook his head. "His regrets are fading quickly. He's looking. Looking at the wolf who killed him. And he feels… He feels only pity. A little bit of envy, of desire is keeping him rooted in place. He wanted a kid with Lexa, you know… Yes… He did. But now he also knows Lexa never loved him like he loved her. Yes, even that regret… That regret is fading."

I watched as the wolf emerged from the hedge a bit more. He didn't make a sound, and neither Chelsea nor King seemed to notice.

"He isn't angry at his killer anymore. He wishes her well—and he has hope she will change." Ginny sighed. "How sweet."

Echo the wolf turned around and took a few steps to walk away. Chelsea's shriek of laughter echoed out into the night and just as Echo was about to reach the hedge again, he turned around, looking up. Maybe at Ginny—like calling to like. But his big, wolf eyes met my gaze, too.

"Rest well, Echo," I whispered. "You were a good man. Faine and I, everyone in your family, your friends and neighbors too—we love you. We'll miss you. Say *hi* to my mom if you see her. She loved you, too. Big brother."

He lifted his muzzle into the air and he howled. The sound, which caught even Chelsea's and King's attention, was melancholy.

But it was sweet and hopeful, too.

King shot to his feet, and I swore he saw the ghost wolf before he vanished into the night.

I hugged Broomie closer to me, tears streaming down my face.

I'd seen him—I'd *felt* him—too. And he would stay with me always.

Join the Spooky Games Club in
Dryads and Dominoes

Spring returns to Luna Lane, and Dahlia Poplar is ready for the turn of the seasons that may bring her long-distance boyfriend back to her by semester's end. Until then, she's doing her best to stay out of the way of the new deputy sheriff after their rocky first impressions of one another. However, a St. Patrick's Day Spooky Games Club event at the town's vampire-run tavern may mean it's time for the town's consulting witch detective to put her sleuthing skills to the test once more.

Vesper the dryad has been the only schoolteacher Luna Lane has ever known. The usually reclusive wood nymph instructor is lured out to the St. Patrick's Day party to help her students construct the largest domino toppling setup the town has ever seen. When a couple of dryads from her past make a surprise appearance at the event, the gentle schoolteacher finds herself accused of murder—and the new deputy sheriff is locking her up and tossing away the key.

Dahlia is certain her former teacher couldn't have committed the crime, but the investigation sets off a chain reaction that seems to build the deputy's case. Before the facts get lost as it all comes toppling down, Dahlia needs to figure out what really happened—but maybe everything isn't as black and white as she thinks.

Witchy Expo Services Mysteries:
Magic, Conventions, and Murder

Witchy Expo Services. We host your convention, expo, or trade show—with a dash of magic!

Set up in a matter of days, our expos can host even the largest of crowds in our witch-run village of Cauldron Cove. We can offer what no other expo planners can: breathtaking illusions, instant teleportation from one end of the center to the other, floating item storage, and all the exceptional, magical touches that will make your event one-of-a-kind. Inquire about Cauldron Cove hosting your next event today by contacting Bernadette Toothaker, award-winning Head Witch General Manager of Witchy Expo Services for eleven decades.

Nimue Toothaker is ecstatic that her world-famous grandmother is about to retire and has chosen her as her successor in the family business. She's only been working on the expos for a few years, but she's confident she has what it takes to lead her fellow witches and warlocks in the business that defines their entire village. Unfortunately, her grandmother's sole condition for Nimue taking the job is that she share the position with her arch rival, an irritating warlock possessed of two minds—quite literally.

First up is Bookshop Con, where indie booksellers from across the nation host authors and sell books to passionate readers. Nimue's grand plans clash with her co-manager's persnickety demands, but their arguments cease to matter when a celebrated author drops dead in the convention center lobby. Nimue suspects murder, but she knows that if she ends the convention prematurely, the magic at work will destroy her beloved hometown. It's a race to catch the killer before they strike again—all while trying to prove she can handle the job she's so desperately always wanted.

About the Author

Amy McNulty is an editor and author of books that run the gamut from YA speculative fiction to contemporary romance. A lifelong fiction fanatic, she fangirls over books, anime, manga, comics, movies, games, and TV shows from her home state of Wisconsin. When not editing her clients' novels, she's busy fulfilling her dream by crafting fantastical worlds of her own.

Sign up for Amy's newsletter to receive news and exclusive information about her current and upcoming projects. Get a free YA romantic sci-fi novelette when you do!

Find her at amymcnulty.com and follow her on social media:

amazon.com/author/amymcnulty

bookbub.com/authors/amy-mcnulty

facebook.com/AmyMcNultyAuthor

twitter.com/mcnultyamy

instagram.com/mcnulty.amy

pinterest.com/authoramymc

Look for More Spectacular Reads
from Crimson Fox Publishing

DARIA WHITE

This won't wash away easily.

Bianca is settling into her new office space, keeping herself occupied for the summer while her daughter visits her ex-husband. Not to mention figuring out

her own personal life now that Detective Sims—
Lamar—asked for a date. It's only a date, though.
What could go wrong? Everything.

When a body in Luther Burkes', her mother's beau,
car wash surfaces, Bianca finds herself wrapped in
another murder case. Is her mother dating a killer?
He is innocent until proven guilty, right?

This case is even more personal for Bianca. Save her
mother from an alleged murderer, or butt heads
with the man who makes her heart skip a beat. Not
a simple choice.

The Alchemy of Sorrow

EDITED BY SARAH CHORN AND VIRGINIA MCCLAIN

Featuring stories by: Sonya M. Black, Angela Boord, Levi Jacobs, Intisar Khanani, Krystle Matar, Virginia McClain, Quenby Olson, Carol A. Park, Madolyn Rogers,

Rachel Emma Shaw, Clayton Snyder, K.S. Villoso, and M. L. Wang.

Here be dragons and sorcery, time travel and sorrow.

Vicious garden gnomes. A grounded phoenix rider. A new mother consumed with vengeance. A dying god. Soul magic. These stories wrestle with the experience of loss—of loved ones, of relationships, of a sense of self, of health—and forge a path to hope as characters fight their way forward.

From bestsellers and SPFBO finalists to rising voices, 13 exceptionally talented authors explore the many facets of grief and healing through the lens of fantasy and sci-fi. In these difficult times, they transform their individual experiences into stories that resonate with audiences who are looking for a touch of magic in their pain.

"From confronting dragons, witches, or monsters, *The Alchemy of Sorrow* may help fight one's inner demons." – Manhattan Book Review